CRAZY ONE MORE TIME

THE ASPEN SERIES

CINDY STARK

OLIVERHEBERBOOKS

Crazy One More Time 2nd Edition© 2023 C. Nielsen

Published by Oliver-Heber Books

0 9 8 7 6 5 4 3 2 1

 Created with Vellum

1

A vivid blood-orange sun hovered close to the horizon as Corey Kendall approached the front door leading into Aspen's Town Hall. Evening shadows played on the sidewalks while lavender lilacs near the front of the building scented the spring air with a sweet perfume.

He stopped and held the door open, waiting for his parents to catch up. Before the city council meeting that night, he'd take an oath and become the newest representative of his small town. He'd be taking his father's spot on the council after health reasons had forced his dad to resign early.

Needless to say, Corey had been thrilled when the town had chosen him as a replacement.

As he waited, the sight of a woman exiting from the passenger side of a rusted blue pickup caught his attention. With silky blond hair and long legs peeking from beneath a fitted black skirt, she was a classic beauty against a piece-of-shit truck. Not unheard of in their part of the country.

The woman turned and leaned back into the vehicle, giving Corey a nice view of her ass. As an upstanding member of the community, he knew he shouldn't stare, but he did anyway. He was single. She appeared to be attractive. It made perfect sense in his world.

Corey's dad took hold of the door, gesturing for Corey's mother and him to step inside. "Come on, son. We need to get you sworn in before the regular meeting starts."

Generations of Corey's family had lived in Aspen, dating back to the late 1800s. Many had served their community in one capacity or another. Now it was his turn to leave a positive mark on the town as well. One that citizens could benefit from for generations.

A small group had gathered in the council's wood-paneled antechamber, including town dignitaries and family members. Corey made his way to the front of the room amidst warm smiles and congratulations, stopping when he stood before the town clerk. Mallory O'Brien's eyes lit with interest as she lifted a black, leather-bound bible and held it out in front of him.

She smiled then, her long, dark hair complementing sapphire eyes. "I'll add my congratulations, Councilman Kendall."

He dipped his head. "Thank you, Mallory."

She'd already celebrated his appointment with him when he'd taken her to dinner in Pinecone Valley the previous week. Polished and refined, she would fit in perfectly with his life's goals. His parents were pressuring him to get married, and he'd always wanted to be a father. Unfortunately, he hadn't discovered that special spark with Mallory, but they hadn't known each other for long, and he was hopeful.

She blinked her long-lashed eyes at him a few times, taking on a serious expression. "Repeat after me. I, Corey Jason Kendall, do solemnly swear to support the Constitution of the United States, the Constitution and Laws of the State of Utah, and the Laws and Ordinances of the City of Aspen, Utah."

He repeated the words before she continued. "I will, to the best of my ability, faithfully perform the duties of council member in the City of Aspen, Utah, during my continuance therein, so help me God."

Confidence, underscored by the need to do a good job, thudded inside his chest as he repeated the oath. Everyone in his long line of ancestors would smile today, including his parents. His dad had been so proud when the town had supported Corey's appointment, and Corey wouldn't let him down.

Larry Downs, the town's other council member, was the first to congratulate him following the brief ceremony. "Welcome aboard. Good to know we have another solid member of the community to protect our interests."

Corey returned his firm handshake, honored to be supported by a man he'd admired for many years. Time had threaded the older man's red hair with white, but his blue eyes still sparkled with intelligence and wit.

"That's right," Mayor Dwight Gardiner said as he, too, shook Corey's hand.

The mayor shared the same potbelly as Larry and Corey's father, though Dwight hadn't been lucky enough to hang onto much of his hair as he'd aged. "We can't let just anybody in the inner circle, you know. We need to ascertain whether a person will uphold our values, protect the better interests of Aspen. I think we've made the right choice."

Corey gave them a nod of reassurance. He wanted to remind the man that the citizens of Aspen had chosen him to serve, not the mayor, but he let it slide. Today was a day for celebration, and he didn't want to start out on the wrong foot. Not to mention, both men had hovered in the background of his childhood, and he'd enjoyed family outings with them and their families. He respected and admired them tremendously. "I'll do my best not to let you down."

"Of course, you will," Dwight said with a wink. "Otherwise, we'd have picked someone else."

Again, an uneasy feeling slid over him, but Larry erased it with a friendly slap on the back. "Let's move this party into the council chambers. We have business to attend to."

A group of over twenty Aspen citizens had already taken their seats in the small meeting room by the time they arrived. Corey followed his fellow representatives inside and took a seat at the long table in front. Someone had placed a placard with his name in front of his seat, along with a crystal glass and a nearby pitcher of water.

He tried not to let the notion of power go to his head, but he couldn't deny he appreciated the prestige. Still, he'd silently vowed to always use his influence for the good of Aspen, and he meant to honor that.

His father sat in the front row alongside his mother, pleased smiles gracing their faces. For the most part, he'd been a dutiful son. He'd studied hard in school and had made good choices. He was proud of the respectable life he'd created. Besides his newest duties, he'd hung up a shingle a year ago, offering architectural services and had done well for a new business.

As Dwight welcomed everyone to the meeting, Corey scanned the rest of the faces, searching for the blonde he'd spotted earlier.

He found her in the back row sitting alongside old man Searle, and his heart faltered in surprise.

It couldn't be.

But it was. After all this time. The one person who'd thrown a wrench into his perfectly planned life. The one who'd tempted him to step outside the box. The one whose kiss he'd never forgotten.

Afton Searle.

She'd left town years ago, and he'd never expected to see her again. But the sight of her had him questioning every future plan he'd made.

Corey stared until her gaze collided with his and held for

several impossibly long seconds. His heart thundered in his chest with excitement. He hoped she would be happy to see him, but understood if she wasn't. Perhaps she still hated him like she had six years ago.

Then she smiled, and the world righted itself.

He could breathe again.

She looked different. No longer a skittish young colt, but a confident woman who held his gaze instead of sneaking shy glances at him.

Attraction coiled inside him like a sleek rattlesnake. He'd tasted her once, and her essence forever lingered in his blood. She wasn't a woman his parents would choose, but that wouldn't stop him from seeking her out now. He needed to know if her hold over him was real or a remnant of an overactive eighteen-year-old imagination.

Her grandfather leaned close to speak to her, and she turned her attention to him.

Johnny Searle looked every bit the outlaw in his old-fashioned suit, wearing a turquoise and silver bolero instead of a tie. He'd drawn his thinning hair into a ponytail, and Corey wouldn't be surprised if he packed a weapon beneath his suit coat.

Corey watched as Afton studied her grandfather's face, listening to him before whispering something in his ear. He'd never personally spoken to Johnny Searle, but his father had condemned the man on more than one occasion for his immoral ways.

What those reasons were, had remained a mystery to him. Sure, Johnny had obviously lived a hard life, but many people in town liked him. Obviously, Afton did, if her expression was a sign.

Her smile could save the devil's soul. She'd been graced with a natural beauty he'd never been able to ignore. If their families hadn't come from such different backgrounds, he wouldn't have been so hesitant to approach her back then.

But the fates had thrown them together for one amazing night. He savored sweet memories of them tangled, naked on the grass beneath a star-filled summer sky. They'd made love and talked until almost sunrise, until his conscience had blasted him with guilt. If only he could keep that one snapshot of time and forget the rest.

They'd both just graduated from high school. He'd been dating straight-A, strait-laced Emily Clinton, but she'd been out of town. He'd reached the point, like he supposed all teenagers did, when he couldn't stand his parents' smothering ways, and he'd tapped into his rebellious streak.

Afton had been soft and willing, tasting of strawberries and her grandfather's whiskey. Unfortunately, a stiff shot of shame had followed. He'd never forgotten their time together. But the guilt of betraying Emily and the cold way he'd treated Afton the following morning were his biggest regrets.

Dwight banged his gavel, jerking Corey's attention to the present.

"Now that we've taken care of the housekeeping business, let's get down to the next item on our agenda. Johnny Searle, you have the floor for five minutes."

2

Afton's stomach clenched as the mayor called her grandfather's name, letting him know it was their turn to speak at the town's council meeting. She hadn't been able to keep her gaze from Councilmember Kendall, and now they'd have to stand and present their case before the man who'd taken her virginity.

Not that her grandfather was aware of her connection to the politician. But on top of the stress of their current situation, Corey's presence made everything more awkward.

Grandpa stood, looking every inch the determined man. Seventy years on earth had taken its toll, casting his dark hair with gray and etching weathered lines on his face. A proud man, he was the hardest worker and most resourceful person she knew.

Afton had been closer to him than she ever had her parents. Her grandpa had given her everything he could. She intended to return the favor by helping him achieve his lifelong dream of opening his own whiskey distillery.

As soon as they could get the damned council to approve their permit, that was.

She stood after he did, prepared to give whatever support he needed.

"Sit down," he whispered. "I can handle this."

She met his gaze head on. "I'm coming. Don't try to stop me."

He cursed under his breath as he walked to the podium. She smiled and followed. No one could deny she'd inherited his tenacity.

He faced the council. "My name is Johnny Searle."

A life full of rough living left his voice scratchy and deep. "I applied for a permit a couple months ago to open a whiskey distillery here in Aspen, where I've lived most of my life. You denied me, Mr. Mayor, and I'm here to appeal."

Mayor Gardiner straightened his tie, taking a moment to puff out his chest before he spoke. "Request denied."

Whispering voices died as undeniable tension spread throughout the courtroom.

Her grandfather leaned close to the microphone. "On what grounds? You haven't heard my appeal yet." His Kentucky-born accent became more pronounced, like it usually did when someone angered him.

A condescending smile pushed out the mayor's fat cheeks. "Aspen is a family-friendly town, Mr. Searle. We denied your request because our citizens would like to keep it that way."

Her grandpa stiffened and cleared his throat while Afton placed a calming hand on his elbow. He released a slow breath, and she hoped he remembered their earlier conversation about retaining his tact.

"What I'm requesting is for a respectable, law-abiding business, Dwight. How does that hurt *our* town?"

Afton noted with surprise that her grandfather had addressed the mayor by his first name. She'd been unaware they'd had a personal connection.

Mayor Gardiner glanced at his fellow council members, gave

them a shared look, and then nodded. "I'm sorry, but alcohol and *good* families don't mix. I believe we've come up against this problem in the past, and, in my opinion, pursuing it doesn't bode well for you." He lifted his brows as though delivering a threat.

Her grandpa held his body straight as he took on the council. "Is that so? Yet, you let Sparrow's stay in business, and they serve alcohol. Plenty of Aspen residents enjoy that establishment, and as far as I can tell, apart from the occasional brawl, no one gets hurt. Some might argue that a place or a way to let off steam, whether it be in town or in the confines of their own homes, is a good thing."

"Not everyone in town agrees Sparrow's should be in business, either," Dwight answered with a little too much force.

Apparently, he wasn't immune to her grandfather's aggressive manner. A showdown between the two, however, wouldn't end well for any of them.

Grandpa inhaled, his face turning red. "Yeah, well, not everyone in town agrees you should make all our decisions, either, you self-righteous son of a—"

Afton covered the microphone, cutting off the rest of his sentence. She narrowed her gaze at her grandpa as he arched an angry brow at her.

She pushed her way between him and the podium. "What my grandfather would like to ask the council is how does he go forward with the appeals process? He has extensive data on how his business will benefit the community by providing jobs and adding to the tax revenue."

Thank God she'd done her research beforehand. "What he's proposed is a small business venture. The processing facility will be on the outskirts of town, nowhere near schools or churches. We believe it will not negatively impact anyone in Aspen in any way."

She paused to smile at each member of the council, hoping

her friendliness would temper her grandpa's caustic manner. When her gaze landed on Corey, an unwanted barb of attraction stung her. Recognition gleamed in his gaze. Then he blinked away their connection to pour himself a glass of water.

Embarrassment nipped her. To this day, she'd never gotten over her one-sided attraction to him. Not that he would ever know.

The mayor focused a steely look at her. "I'm sorry, Miss..."

She held his gaze without blinking. "Afton Searle."

He gave her a fake smile and dipped his head. "The council has already discussed and decided the appeal's matter. It's been denied."

She'd heard Mayor Gardiner was a pig-headed jerk, but she'd never experienced his behavior first-hand until now. "But you haven't let us fully present our case. I'm sure if we hired an attorney and took the matter to court, a judge would agree you should hear us out before you decide."

Afton inhaled a calming breath, refusing to follow her grandfather and allow the mayor to fluster her. "Don't you think it would be better to let the citizens of Aspen choose? If you're certain they'll go against us, then what can it matter if we petition them for their opinion?"

She turned her gaze to the redheaded councilman, since he seemed to be the most neutral party.

Mr. Downs shifted in his chair, taking a moment to consider her proposition. "I expect I would be okay with that."

The mayor jerked his surprised gaze in the councilmember's direction, while Corey's eyes lit with amused interest. Perhaps the mayor hadn't been speaking for all of them after all.

When Corey glanced her way, she sent him a questioning look, asking if he'd support her or not. She had no idea how he'd respond, but she hoped he'd be more cordial to her than he had in the past.

He gave her the barest nod before he turned to the Mayor. "I agree that we should allow Ms. Searle and her grandfather to collect signatures. Seems we should know who supports their endeavor before we completely dismiss the application."

Corey adjusted his tie. "There are two-hundred fifty-five residents in Aspen, and two-thirds of them are old enough to vote. If Ms. Afton and her father can collect, say one hundred signatures, roughly sixty percent of the voting population, I believe we should take another look at their proposal. Otherwise, as you stated, Mr. Mayor, the appeal is a moot point."

Mayor Gardiner's face flamed bright red as he stared down at Corey. He seemed to be angrier with him than he'd been with Mr. Downs. "Is that so? Well. Since it appears my two counterparts agree, we'll give you a month to collect your signatures, Mr. and Ms. Searle."

"One month?" Afton asked with a gasp. That would be next to impossible. "We would ask for a minimum of three months."

The mayor gave her a crafty smile. "You have until our next council meeting to present your petition. If the town supports you like you believe they will, you should have no problem."

He banged his gavel. "Moving to the next item on the agenda."

Afton shot a fiery look at the mayor, but took her grandfather's elbow before he exploded. "Don't worry," she whispered. "We'll make it happen."

"Damn right," he said as he opened the chamber doors and followed her out of the room into the evening.

———

Dwight's disapproval boomed from him, echoing off the paneled walls of the council's antechamber as the three governing members entered. "What on God's green earth did you hope to accomplish, giving that scourge Searle the go-ahead, Larry?"

Larry shrugged his thin shoulders. "I don't know. It seemed like a good thing. We don't want them taking us to court. Taxpayers wouldn't like that one bit."

Dwight stepped closer to him. "Of all the people to be swayed by a nice ass and a good pair of tits. I expected better of you."

Larry firmly closed the door behind them. "Mind your words, Dwight. It's an election year for me, all right? God dammit. I have other things to consider besides catering to your sorry ass."

Dwight's face deepened to a darker shade of red, and he shot a venomous look at Larry. "Don't god dammit, me." Then he turned to Corey. "I rue the day Martin Kendall resigned. I could always count on his support."

Larry rounded on him. "Like you didn't get my support all those years ago with the Banfield deal? Not to mention multiple times since?"

Corey widened his eyes, shocked to hear his father's two oldest friends, men he highly respected, speaking in such a manner. "Excuse me. But I don't believe we should discuss Miss Searle's assets."

Dwight redirected his anger at Corey. "We need to have a talk, *son*. From our previous discussions, I thought I'd made our expectations perfectly clear. Not to mention, I'm certain your father talked to you."

He hoped the mayor wasn't insinuating he assumed complete and utter submission. "Your expectations?"

"Mine. Your father's," he said with a pointed look. "Everyone knows old Johnny has been illegally distilling for years. We've tried to shut him down many times. But the sheriff isn't willing to invest any more personnel than he already has to bring him down. Especially since it's such a small operation, and they can't pinpoint the exact location of the still."

Larry eyed him. "Sounds like the sheriff has better things to do with his limited budget and resources."

Dwight continued talking as if he hadn't heard Larry. "My nephew does his best to investigate when he has cause to be in the area, but the wilderness around Searle's house is expansive. Can you imagine my disgrace if suddenly we legitimized his operation?"

Corey exhaled a calming breath, hoping it would spread to the rest of the occupants in the room. "Don't make it personal, Dwight. That old man isn't out to make you look bad. He just wants what he wants. It's not about you."

Dwight placed a hand on his thick chest and took a deep breath. "The hell it isn't. He's wanted my neck for years, and you and Larry are ready to hand it to him on a silver platter."

Larry shoved a chair in his direction. "Sit down before you have a heart attack, Dwight."

The mayor glared, but lowered himself onto the seat.

Corey scrubbed a hand over the short whiskers on his chin. Why would Afton's grandfather give a shit about a stuffy old councilmember? "Honestly, I don't believe that's what this is all about."

Dwight clenched his jaw.

Corey ignored him like the mayor had done with Larry. "Either way, you should know I'll vote my conscience. I'm sorry if you thought I would do otherwise. Larry said the right thing. Let her collect signatures. You've set her up to fail as it is, so really, you have nothing to worry about."

"If this goes through, our constituents will *not* be happy." Dwight shook his head, a few wisps of hair falling from his comb-over to slither over his mottled forehead. "Mark my words, boy. This won't end well."

3

Afton sat in the passenger seat of her grandfather's old truck, darkness surrounding them, as she inwardly fumed at the mayor's treatment. Her grandpa hadn't lost his anger as he drove them toward his home in the hills, deep within the pines and aspens a few miles from the center of town. His jaw remained hard, and he hadn't spoken to her since they'd left the courthouse.

She'd let him be for now, knowing it would take time before he'd cool down and regain his head. He'd always carried a chip on his shoulder regarding the authorities in town, always said they were out to get him. She'd never really believed it until now.

Many cities and towns issued licenses to craft distillers. She couldn't discover a single reason the mayor and council members would deny his permit. As it was, her grandpa supplied half the town with the occasional bottle of his own Sagecreek Whiskey, anyway.

Unless the mayor's denial *was* something personal against him.

"Thanks for coming with me, dumplin'," Grandpa said through the quiet.

A weight eased off her, and the crisis had passed. She shifted in her seat, facing him. "You don't need to thank me. This is my dream, too. We're going to do this, you know? Or make them give us a legal reason we can't."

Grandpa sighed. "I've been thinking on the way home, and I don't want to take it too far. Let's see what they'll do with a little shove. Nothing big."

She snorted. "If I shove them, it's not going to be little. I'll take them all the way to the Supreme Court or the Governor's office if I must."

"No." His clipped reply bounced off the truck's interior. "I don't want to do that."

Afton folded her arms. "Why not? For years, we've talked about owning a legitimate distillery. You're the one who sold me on your dream. I'm not about to let an egotistical politician get in my way. I can't believe you would, either."

He turned off the main highway and onto the road that would lead them to her grandpa's secluded home. The truck bumped over a familiar rock in the dirt road, making them bounce in their seats. "I'm getting too old for this shit."

She scoffed. "You are not." If nothing else, she'd always been able to count on his strength and conviction.

"Don't sass me. It's like I said, I've had time to think it over. I don't want a big fight."

It wasn't like him to cave so easily. "Adults don't sass. They ask questions, for your information."

He sent her a sideways glance as a warning. "Sounds like sassing to me."

But she wouldn't give up that easily. She also wouldn't allow him to treat her like a child. They were about to become business partners, and he needed to see her as an equal. "I've never seen you back down from a fight, especially not over something important. The council needs to give serious consideration to our appeal, and I'm going to make sure they do. I don't know what Gardiner has stuck up his ass, but there's something."

He snorted. "Ain't that the truth? He's had it up there for years."

She eyed him, wondering again about a personal connection between him and the mayor. "I don't understand why they would care. It's not like we're going to increase production to hundreds of bottles a month and corrupt the good citizens of Aspen by forcing whiskey down their throats. The people here are already purchasing bottles of it. Why not legitimize the business and increase revenue?"

She'd never approved of what he did for extra income, but how could she bite the hand that fed her? Now was their chance to make everything good and above-board.

Her grandfather coughed, and once he started, it took him a moment to regain control. Afterward, he spoke in a raspy voice. "Should have stopped smoking years ago."

She'd worried about the state of his lungs for a while now, but he always insisted he was okay. "Have you seen the doctor for that cough?"

He waved away her concern. "I have. It's nothing that time won't cure."

His reply brought relief and allowed her to not feel guilty for pressing the issue. He'd thought he'd changed the subject, but she wasn't finished with their conversation yet. "Gardiner must know you make whiskey. It's never been a tightly kept secret. They all must know. I don't understand why they're fighting it. Why not give you the opportunity to be legitimate?"

"Let it go, dumplin'." His graveled voice made the term even more endearing, but she wouldn't let it sway her.

"I'm not going to let it go."

The fact that he didn't seem willing to fight bothered her the most. She couldn't see him give up. That would mean he'd grown too tired to fight, and that wasn't acceptable in her book. She needed him to be strong and capable. She still wanted him around for a damn long time, even though she could now take care of herself without his help.

He pulled up next to the house, and a yellow glow from the porch burned its way through the thick trees to welcome them home. "I said, let it go. It's my fight, and I get the final say."

Afton gathered her files and purse. "I think we should sit at the table and review our strategy."

She braced for a stronger reaction, but he shook his head and smiled instead. "You remind me of her, you know. Your grandmama?"

His recurring comment always brought a smile to her face. "I know. I also know she was a sassy lady who no one dared to argue with, so you should listen to me. We've planned this for years. I pursued a degree in business so I could help you. Your dream became mine, and I can't walk away so easily."

They exited the truck and fell into step beside each other as they walked to the house, the cool spring air nipping at their faces. When she opened the front door, the newest love of her life danced and wagged his cute puppy tail in excitement.

Afton kneeled on the green rug inside and rubbed Sonny's ears. "Hello, beautiful."

The sweet golden retriever pup whined to let her know how happy he was to see her. She would only be his foster mommy for a while, but until she found someone to love him as much as she did, she'd make sure he had the best home ever.

"It's not just your sass that reminds me of her, you know." Grandpa smiled as he stepped inside and closed the door behind them. "She was beautiful, like you, but she also possessed an irresistible charm that many couldn't refuse."

"What are you talking about? You could hardly call my long

arms and gangly legs beautiful." She straightened. "And stop trying to change the subject."

"I guaran-damn-tee we wouldn't have gotten the go-ahead for a petition if you hadn't smiled at them the way you did. You carry some clout, dumplin', even if you don't realize it."

She shook her head, though his flattery warmed her. "You have to say that because you're my grandpa."

He laughed, the sound resonant and very welcome. "That may be, but I know what I'm talking about. You don't get to be my age and not learn a thing or two."

She wasn't intentionally goading him to draw him into action, but she needed to know he hadn't lost his fire. "Then tell me this. If one thing you taught me was not to give up on what I want or love, why are you giving up so easily? Seems like a cowardly thing to me."

He chuckled and shook his head. "You're definitely a spitfire. Just like she was."

She'd never known her grandmother. She'd died shortly after Afton's father had been born, but she loved hearing the stories. "I take after both of you."

Her grandpa rarely spoke of her father, nor the woman his son had impregnated. Afton barely remembered her parents other than they yelled a lot, smoked a lot, and left her alone a lot. She'd wanted to die the day they'd dumped her on her grandpa's doorstep, but it had turned out to be the best thing for her.

Grandpa paused and stared at her for a moment. "Okay. Fine. We'll go ahead with the petition. But only because you want it so badly. 'Sides, someone needs to show those assholes where to shit in the woods."

Thankfully, passion for life still burned deep within him, after all. The effort needed to collect so many signatures would be an uphill battle, but she was ready to fight for her future.

"Yes!" She threw her arms around his neck. "We can do this. I know we can. People here will support you. The mayor doesn't know what he's talking about. Also, I'm working on a list of ingredient suppliers, but I'm not sure about all the equipment. We should go over that."

He lifted a hand. "Whoa. Slow down, dumplin'. I think we'd better get the go ahead first."

She grinned. "Don't worry, Grandpa. I know what I'm doing. I want to be ready when the council approves our business permit."

An hour later, Afton was still anxious and unable to stop her mind from processing how she'd get everything to work in her favor. To distract herself, she'd checked email and corresponded with the woman who ran the pet shelter in Pinecone. Still no interest in Sonny, which was fine with her. She enjoyed having the friendly dog around and knew it wouldn't be long before someone snatched him up.

As part of a first-year college class requirement, she'd volunteered at a pet rescue organization. There, she'd developed a passion for helping homeless animals. She knew very well what it was like to go hungry and to not have a safe place to sleep, and she'd decided then to do what she could to help.

She'd remained involved ever since, stopping by the shelter in Pinecone the day after she'd moved home to offer her services as a foster mom.

But that distraction had only taken her so far tonight. Sonny had long since passed out at her feet after running himself into exhaustion, so he was no help. She couldn't stand the waiting and wondering. She needed to *do* something.

With a sigh, she pulled out her to-do list for their soon-to-be business. Once they secured their business license, she could open the checking account. She'd already filed papers to make their LLC legal.

Unfortunately, she couldn't do anything with equipment until her grandpa sat down with her, but he wanted to wait. Everything from this point forward hinged on gaining their business license.

"Dammit." She honestly couldn't understand why the mayor had to be such a jerk.

To appease her restless spirit, Afton opened a blank document on her laptop and created the petition they'd use. She printed out copies, ten pages of empty lines. That was all that stood between her and her future.

Well, that and the ability to launch a new business, but that part didn't scare her. She'd have control over that situation. The council's approval? Not so much.

Thoughts of the council led to Corey. She had no idea what he thought of her and her grandpa's endeavor or if he cared at all. At first, she'd wondered if he'd remember her, but knowing had blazed in his eyes, stirring the longing from her past.

She wished she could pretend she didn't still think of him from time to time. Wished more that he didn't still affect her. She'd grown up and had gotten over the hurt of rejection, so she couldn't fathom why one look from him could resurrect such powerful feelings of longing.

She really needed to get over herself, and fast.

Afton set the petition pages on her desk and stood, but she couldn't walk away. The pages leered at her, taunting her with their empty spaces. She signed her name on the first line, but that didn't help.

What are you waiting for, they seemed to ask.

"Nothing," she said, not questioning why she talked to the papers. "I'm not waiting for anything."

In fact, she'd start now. Sparrow's would still be open, and she was bound to find several supporters there. If she headed out now, she could have a great head start on securing her future before she went to bed that night.

With her decision made, Afton tiptoed out of her room so she wouldn't wake Sonny. And she made sure her grandpa's bedroom door was open in case the pup woke and was lonely.

Then she headed out to stake a claim on her dream.

4

Afton pushed through the front doors of Sparrow's Bar and Grill, primed and ready to make her mark on the world. The cool, dim atmosphere greeted her, along with a slow country song that echoed from the jukebox, though no one danced on the wooden floor. Less than half the tables had occupants, and Afton glanced around, searching for a familiar face. When she spotted Sam Peterson at the bar, she claimed the seat next to him.

Sam lifted his glass in a toast. "Well, if it isn't Miss Afton, back from the big city."

Her heart lightened. "Hi, Sam."

She'd always loved her grandfather's friend, from his thick silver mustache, to the drawl in his voice. "You know, for as long as I've known you, I don't think you've ever told me where you grew up."

The cowboy lifted one side of his mouth into a lopsided smile. "Texas. Lubbock. Hub of the Plains."

"How on earth did you end up in small-town Utah?"

He patted her hand, the scent of whiskey from his breath filling the space between them. "A woman."

She chuckled. "I should have known. With you, it's always women."

Afton glanced at the bartender, happy to see one of her good friends. "Hey, Becky. I'll take a shot of your best bourbon, neat."

"It's not me," Sam continued as Becky poured. "They're the ones always breaking *my* heart. Still, I can't stay away."

Becky snorted. "That's the problem, Sam. If you try to have more than one at a time, the ladies tend not to like that so much."

He dipped his head. "True, true. And I always say I'm done with that, but then a real sweetheart walks in, and I can't help myself."

Afton couldn't keep the smile from her face. "One day the right lady will come, and you'll be so smitten, you won't want to look at another."

"That's right," Becky said as she delivered Afton's drink. "When that day comes, you'll never live it down."

Sam grinned. "Maybe you'll fall for me, Becky."

"Too late." She held up her hand, flashing a small diamond. "Already married."

He lifted a seductive brow. "Since when does a ring stop anything?"

"Never if we're talking about you." Becky winked and walked away.

Afton lifted her drink and sipped, allowing the taste of the alcohol to tickle her tongue. A sweet, honey-tinged flavor filled her mouth before she swallowed and allowed the smooth drink to slide down her throat. The finish was just as good as the first. "Lovely," she murmured.

Sam adjusted his hat. "Wish your grandpa would take up bourbon. If he could make it as good as his whiskey, you'd be rich."

"He doesn't want to be rich, Sam. Just legitimate."

The cowboy nodded. "I heard about the meeting tonight."

The reminder dimmed her good mood. "Yeah, he got hot-headed, like he does sometimes, and set off the tension in the room." She sighed. "He may not be perfect, Sam, but he's perfect to me, you know? I only want to see him happy."

He gave her a commiserating grin. "Hey, a bunch of us were talking about it earlier. We'd be happy to sign your petition."

She pulled out the papers and a pen and set them before him. "Perfect. Here you go then."

He hailed Becky and another customer at the bar to have them sign, too.

Now she had four names, including hers. "Thank you. I was counting on that. With the town's support, I feel like we can make it happen."

"Damn right," Sam said. "We'll stand behind him."

She leaned over and put an arm around his shoulders. "Thank you for that. I appreciate it so much."

Sam smoothed his bushy mustache with a thumb and forefinger. "If me and your grandpa weren't such good friends, I'd be taking my chances on you."

Afton laughed. As if he'd have anything close to a shot. "Good thing, then. I don't think I could stand it if you broke my heart, too."

He gave a hearty guffaw. "Damn, Afton, you're good for an old man's ego."

A cool breeze wafted in, and they both turned to see who'd entered the bar. Afton recognized Jerry Tierno's tall, muscled frame, but she'd never met the man who accompanied him.

At least it wasn't Corey. He and Jerry had been inseparable years ago, and she wondered if they'd remained friends.

As the men made their way to the back of the bar, Jerry lifted his brows as though surprised to see her and acknowledged her with a nod.

Afton returned the greeting, remembering again the time after graduation and the secret party on a remote section of Grandpa's property. She'd been stupid and wild and crazy, and she'd given her virginity to a guy she barely knew. Seemed such an insane thing to do now that she was older, but at the time, she hadn't cared.

She wondered if Corey had ever told Jerry about seducing her under the stars, or if it remained a secret. The morning after, she'd been too ashamed to tell her friends and to this day, she'd never shared with anyone.

Her thoughts shifted directions. If Jerry *had* remained friends with Corey, he might have some pull with the councilmember. Since Corey had a say in the outcome of her future, it might not be a bad idea to convince Jerry, and from there, Corey, to support their cause.

"Excuse me," Afton said to Sam as she stood from her stool, taking her drink with her. "I need to say hi to an old friend and see if I can get one more signature."

Regret hit hard the moment she stepped into the back room. Jerry and his friend sat huddled at a table, whispering something to none other than Corey. To make matters worse, the three of them were the only people in that section of the bar, so it wasn't as though she could pretend that she'd meant to talk with someone else.

Before she could escape unnoticed, Jerry turned and gestured toward the front of the bar. He froze when he spotted her, looking guilty as his hand hovered in midair, and all eyes turned to her. She had no doubt she'd been the topic of conversation.

Corey still wore the white button-down shirt he'd had on earlier, but he'd lost the tie. Instead, he'd rolled up his sleeves, revealing muscular forearms.

She concentrated on breathing as a tremor of attraction rolled through her. When she'd been all buttoned up at the council meeting, in a room full of others, including her grandpa, Corey hadn't seemed as dangerous.

A shadowy bar, intimate with only a few people around, left her much more vulnerable.

Her bold idea to confront Corey in the distant future and ask him to back her grandfather dissipated. She became, once again, the gangly girl who'd dared to flirt with a handsome boy at the party so she wouldn't be the only one of her friends who was still a virgin.

For a wonderful moment in time that night, she hadn't been the girl from the wrong side of town. She'd felt beautiful, wanted, and they'd talked of amazing things as she'd snuggled in his arms. He'd had lofty goals for the future, and a depth to his thoughts that surprised her.

It wasn't until the next morning when she realized he'd regretted every second with her. Worse, she was damn sure he hadn't understood she'd given him her innocence. He'd been too drunk to notice.

"Uh, sorry. Didn't mean to interrupt." She swiveled on her heels and headed away from them as fast as she could without running.

"Afton, wait!"

The sound of Corey calling her name speared her. She halted, though she wanted to continue walking, and closed her eyes. She wasn't prepared for a one-on-one meeting.

When she sensed Corey behind her, she pasted on a fake smile to hide her mortification and turned. Immediately, powerful attraction struck her.

Standing right next to him, she found he was taller than she remembered. His eyes were a perfect shade of midnight, his body hard and lean and so tempting. He'd had the rebelliousness clipped from his hair, leaving him clean-cut and respectable. But that hadn't done anything to erase how he affected her.

She considered pretending she didn't remember him, but couldn't. She held out a hand for him to shake, as though they might have been old friends. "How are you, Corey?"

He accepted her friendly gesture as a flash of intrigue fired in his gaze. "I'm well. You?"

He kept hold of her hand, sending an influx of heated currents into her fingers and palm. She cleared her throat and slipped her hand from his. "Other than the outcome of today's meeting, I'm good."

An embarrassed smile curved his lips, and he glanced toward his friends. "Yeah, it's not the best way to reconnect with you after all this time, is it?"

Reconnect? Like they'd had something more than one night in the grass on a hillside under the stars. Like their deep conversation that night hadn't been a way for him to get into her panties. "Right."

Awkwardness slipped over her like a hangman's noose, and she struggled for a better reply. Instead, she took a drink of bourbon, not stopping until it was gone.

Then coughed.

He laughed. "It can't be worse than your grandpa's moonshine."

The case of whiskey she and Laurel had discovered in her grandpa's barn had been the harshest she'd ever tasted. "Oh, God, no."

Corey's eyes brightened. "How much do you think we drank that night?"

That night? She'd been so certain she'd left that night in the past where it belonged.

"Too much," she said, the bourbon helping her to regain some of her fire. His over-friendly words and actions confused her, and she couldn't pretend otherwise any longer. "If I remember correctly, I threw up, and you couldn't have been in a bigger hurry to leave the next morning when you woke up with me in your arms."

"Ouch." He placed a hand over his heart. "I suppose I deserved that."

She held up a hand, determined to stop their reminiscing before it went any further. She wouldn't do this here. Wouldn't do it now...or ever. She'd moved on. "Don't worry about it, Corey. That was so many years ago that I hardly remember. Besides, we have more important things to think about, don't you agree?"

Her refusal to buy into his pretend friendliness increased her sense of power. "You're with your buddies right now, so I won't press this issue. But maybe in the next couple of days, if you have a few moments, I'd like to speak with you about my grandfather's appeal."

There. Keep it cool and professional.

He gave her an unexpected smile. "I'd like that. Why don't you stop by my office tomorrow around four-thirty or five?"

Just like that, the noose tightened around her neck, and she had no way to escape. "That would be great. I'd appreciate your time."

A sparkle lit in his eyes. "Perfect. I look forward to it."

With her insides trembling, she took her leave, setting her empty glass on a vacant table as she made a beeline for the exit before her past could trip her up once again.

5

Corey studied the document on his computer screen, ignoring the fact it was already mid-morning. He should be drafting plans for the new administrative building in Pinecone, but he'd wanted a closer look at the Searle appeal. So far, it appeared they had everything in order, and he couldn't help wondering if the mayor realized they stood on very shaky ground by denying the Searle's permit.

The sound of his front door opening drew Corey's gaze upward. He operated his business out of his home, and it wasn't unusual for people to pop in during the day. He clicked the electronic copy of their appeal closed and stood as his father and Dwight Gardiner entered.

"Hey, Dad." Corey shook his father's hand like always. "Mayor." He repeated the same greeting. "What brings you out this way today?"

"Nothing much, son," his dad said. "Dwight and I are headed into Pinecone for a round of golf. Thought you might like to join us."

"Isn't it too early in the season?" Corey asked with a grin. He knew as well as anyone that the moment the layer of winter snow disappeared, the fairways were fair game to his dad.

Dwight chuckled, his anxiety from the previous night seeming to be a distant memory. "You know your dad, Corey. Soon as the snow melts..."

He grinned, relieved to be at ease around the two men. "So true."

Then Dwight gave his dad a pointed look, pulling the tension strings tight once again.

His father sat in a leather visitor chair across from Corey's desk. "Son, we need to talk." Dwight lowered his portly body into the seat next to him, his expression equally serious.

Corey held his tongue as he resumed his seat behind the large walnut desk. He'd listen before he told them to back off.

"Dwight and I are sorely disappointed in Larry's and your actions last night." His father steepled his fingers, adopting the expression he'd used when Corey had been an errant child. "You're putting the whole town at risk, and our mayor depends on you both for support."

"At risk? For what? Democracy?" He didn't enjoy using a flippant tone with either of them, but they'd asked for it.

His father drew his brows together, not pleased with his answer.

"Let's not make jokes here," Dwight cautioned.

"I'm not joking. Far from it." Corey tilted his head, wondering how he could have missed this part of his father and his friends all these years. "The Searles presented a valid appeal. It's our duty to hear it."

"*The Searles*," Dwight repeated with disdain. "Johnny Searle is nothing but a no-good felon in sheep's clothing. Then, his granddaughter thinks she can come into my chambers and make demands as if she owns the place. I won't tolerate it."

"As well, you shouldn't," his father agreed. "The citizens of this town need to know who's in control."

Corey choked on their words. "Whoa, gentlemen. Are you hearing yourselves? You sound like fascist, radical leaders. We're voted in by the people to represent them, not to lord our personal views over them. The Searles deserve the same respect as everyone else in this town."

His father cleared his throat. "Corey, I understand your point, but please recognize you are new to this position. You may need some time before you can appreciate the tough job of being a councilmember. The townsfolk want two things from us: safety and a way to make a decent living. When something threatens either of those two things, it's our job to speak out."

Except he saw no evidence of threats. "I agree, especially with wanting to make a decent living, which is exactly what the Searles are asking for. What they want is perfectly within legal boundaries. The state approved their application, and we're obligated to hear them."

Dwight snorted. "Legal boundaries, possibly. But what about moral ones?"

Corey wasn't sure he could argue with that aspect. "Either way, we need to follow due process. It's the best approach. The legal, moral choice will win."

The mayor studied Corey with a scrutinizing, condescending look on his face. "Now I understand."

Corey braced himself for an impending attack. "Understand what?"

Dwight leaned closer. "Have you slept with her, son? Because I understand the complexities of sex and how that can mess with a man's mind and his priorities. God knows, she's pretty enough, and that's the only reason I can think of why you're refusing to support me on this."

Fire raced through Corey's veins, and he stood abruptly. "You're out of line."

Corey's dad held up his palms as though that would keep the other two from coming to blows. "Hold on, boys. Let's keep this civil. Dwight, that might be taking things too far."

The mayor calmed his features into a docile politician's smile. "If so, I beg your pardon, Corey. I'm only trying to understand where you're coming from and what it will take to get you on board with the rest of the council...and the town, for that fact."

Dwight inhaled. "Think about it, Corey. These good family people don't want a distillery in their quiet little town. They go to church. They have children. They want peace, prosperity, and goodness."

Corey resumed his seat, also wanting to keep the discussion from escalating further. "I understand that. I want those things for the town, too. But I believe everyone has the right to be heard, and I believe in fairness for all. I think we should keep our personal biases out of decisions."

Dwight nodded. "You're right, of course. We should. I apologize if it seemed I wasn't. But, as your daddy can tell you, I nearly always share the opinion of my constituents. That's all I meant to express, not to mention saving us some time reviewing an appeal when the outcome won't change. I expect the longer you hold office, the more you'll come to realize the same."

"Fine." Corey's respiration calmed, though he wasn't entirely convinced of Dwight's motives. "Apology accepted."

His dad leaned closer to the desk. "You're not sleeping with her, are you?" he asked in low tones.

"*Seriously?*" He gave his father a disappointed look that would rival the ones he'd received as a child. "No, I'm not sleeping with her."

No need to mention he had once in the past. That had no bearing on the current situation at all.

"She's pretty enough to want to, so I would understand if you did," his dad said, and Corey shot him a disturbed look. "But you have your eye on that O'Brien girl, and she's the one you want standing behind you. Like I've always said, keep the whores hidden in the backroom and the presentable wife out front."

Their conversation had taken an unsettling turn for the worse, and he was appalled by his father's behavior. "Wow, Dad, really? Since when have you had a whore in the backroom?"

His father had the decency to blush. "It's just a metaphor, son."

Dwight stood. "I hope you'll think about what I said, Corey. I understand the romantic notion of fighting for justice, but really, the taxpayers don't want us to waste their dollars. Are you sure you can't join us for golf? It's going to be a beautiful day."

Corey bit back his initial reply. "Thanks, but no. I have work to finish. I appreciate the invitation, though."

"Good enough." His father stood and held out a hand to shake. "We'll see you later, son. Don't forget to call your momma. She's expecting you for dinner one night this week."

Corey watched the two men walk from his office, replaying their interaction in his mind. They'd come because they feared his future actions, and they'd left, seeming assured of them. But really, nothing had changed. At least not in his mind.

He'd vote his conscience according to what was fair and just to the citizens of Aspen. He sure as hell wouldn't be swayed by some old boys' club secret code.

Who the hell did they think they were?

More importantly, who the hell did they believe *he* was?

———

Afton shook out her hands as she slowly approached Corey's front gate, as if that would dispel her nerves. When she'd agreed to meet him at his office, she'd assumed it would be somewhere in town.

Not at his *home*.

She glanced down at her soft white sweater and newest jeans, suddenly feeling very underdressed. She should have gone with slacks and her leather jacket. But then she might be overdressed.

The front gate opened without a sound, allowing her entrance into his well-groomed yard. Red tulips and yellow daffodils along the edges of the walk leading to his house danced in the breeze. Pink blossoms dripped from several weeping cherry trees in the front gardens, transporting her into a land of lush beauty.

In comparison, the grass at her house might go a couple of weeks without mowing, and the flowers were remnants of bulbs someone had planted at one time. Still, her childhood home had a wonderful wildness about it, like a beautiful, untamed stallion roaming the plains.

She liked to think it might be how the pioneers had first viewed the valley when they'd settled the area. Nothing wrong with that.

Afton exhaled as she stood in front of the gorgeous wooden door and lifted her finger to press the bell. The sound of chimes echoed through the house.

Her nerves hovered on the edge, and she quickly wiped her hands on her jeans while she waited. The sound of the doorknob turning sent her heart rate spiraling upward.

Corey opened the door, looking better than a man ever should. His gray cotton shirt was open at the neck, his sleeves rolled up to reveal those forearms she loved to see. His dark hair looked ruffled, as though he'd run his fingers through it many times, and his midnight eyes pierced her to the core.

She swallowed.

"Afton." He smiled warmly, tugging at all the tender strings inside her. "Please come in."

6

Afton returned Corey's greeting and stepped into his home, her heels connecting with the hardwood floor, making a deep, resonating sound. Dark, rich woods and ivory walls added to the luxurious feel, reminding her, once again, the differences between their two lifestyles.

"You've done well for yourself," she said as she followed him into the office near the front door. "Your home is beautiful."

He glanced about the room, a satisfied look in his eyes. "Thank you. I've restored most of it myself."

She took a second look, impressed with his talents. "Really?"

He gestured toward one of the cushioned leather chairs across from his desk. "Does that surprise you?"

She sat, trying to pretend she wasn't very aware of his proximity, nor the enticing scent of his cologne. "I can't say I know you well enough to make a determination either way, though you didn't seem like someone who'd enjoy that kind of work."

He took the seat next to her instead of making his way to the chair behind the desk, which left her with no barriers to protect her. "I don't?"

"I didn't mean to insult you," she said, trying to backtrack her obvious blunder. "But I didn't think you were the type to get his hands dirty."

He lifted his brows higher.

She'd often been judged harshly because of her family circumstances, and she exhaled the hypocritical air from her lungs. "Sorry. I should stop now. I cringe when people make assumptions like that, yet here I am doing the same."

He chuckled and grinned. "No apology needed. You're entitled to speak your mind."

Corey ran his gaze over her in what he surely meant as a casual glance, but it sent shivers racing across her skin. She squashed her feelings as if they were a venomous spider and gave him a hopeful smile. "Still, it's not a smart way to begin a conversation when one wants to ask for a favor."

He returned the friendly gesture, the curve of his sensuous mouth drawing her attention. "Is that what this is about? I'd wondered."

She remembered those lips, the way he'd possessed hers, how soft and yet how powerful they'd been. Six years had passed, and she still remembered.

Afton blinked and returned her gaze to his eyes, finding him watching her with a curious expression. "I'd hoped there might be something you could do to help my grandpa with his appeal."

He leaned back in his chair, regarding her with an interested look. "Such as?"

She shrugged. "I don't know. Maybe talk to the mayor and the other council member, and see if they'll extend the time we have to collect signatures. You know as well as I do, Mayor Gardiner purposefully cut it short."

Corey shook his head and sighed. "I wish I could help, but I doubt I can convince him to change his mind. He's determined to deny your appeal, but at least you have your chance."

He shifted in his seat. "Just curious, but is there bad blood between him and your grandpa? I've never seen the mayor get so worked up."

She'd wondered the same thing the previous night. "Not that I know of."

"Hmm..." He placed a hand on her forearm, causing high-wattage shivers to shoot through her. "My best advice would be to see what you can accomplish during the next few weeks. As much as Mayor Gardiner would hate to hear it, I believe your grandpa has more support than he realizes. Also, if you decide you need it, I can connect you with someone who can give you pointers on how to rally people to your cause."

Her heart warmed. "Really? You would do that for my grandfather?"

He met her gaze head on. "I don't know your about grandfather, but I would do that for *you*." Once again, the strings of attraction tightened. "What's your phone number?"

She tried to draw a logical line of conclusion from his offer to help, to needing her phone number, but couldn't. "My number?"

"So I can text her contact information to you." He pulled his phone from his pocket as if to prove his intent.

"Oh. Sure." She recited her number as embarrassment churned inside. "Thank you so much for doing this."

He tapped his phone, and hers chimed with an incoming message. She glanced down, saw that it was from him, and blinked away the awkward feeling. If that would have happened years earlier, she would have been giddy.

Before she could thank him again, his phone rang. His gaze bounced awkwardly between it and her, as though he wondered if he should answer it.

"Excuse me for a moment." He stood and walked outside the office door.

"Hey," he said as his voice grew lower the farther he moved away.

Afton stayed seated, trying not to listen to his conversation. She studied the gorgeous painting hanging behind his desk instead. The artist had depicted the beautiful rolling hills of Aspen with the sharp mountains rising behind them. It reminded her so much of her grandfather's property. He had another of George Washington and his horse surrounded by trees. Along with those, he had shelves full of books, many of them fiction.

Corey's voice echoed from the hallway. "I'm sorry I won't be able to make dinner tonight. I know we tentatively had plans, but something's come up. I have a project I need to focus on. It's important. Can you forgive me?"

Another long pause. For whatever reason, he was canceling his dinner date with someone. "Okay, good. Thanks for under-standing. I'll call soon."

Just as Corey reentered the room, Afton glanced at the first painting straight ahead of her, as though she hadn't been surveying his office. This time, she caught sight of a small shack in the painting, barely noticeable among the pine trees, and she narrowed her gaze to study it better.

The painter *had* captured part of her grandpa's land. The wooden structure wasn't far from where she and her best friend had held that wild, end-of-summer party where Corey had first kissed her, where he'd...

"I recognize the area in that painting," she said as he resumed his seat.

A sparkle lit in his eyes. "Do you?"

She studied it. "It's the north part of my grandpa's property. Beautiful painting. Do I know the artist?"

He pointed his thumbs at his chest as he tried to subdue his smile.

His response shocked her. "You painted that?"

She stood and moved behind the desk for a closer look. "I'm impressed. How did you make it so perfect?" When she turned, she found him only inches behind her, also looking up at the painting, and she shivered.

He dropped his gaze to her. "That's twice in one day that I've caught you off guard with my answers. That leaves me to think you haven't had a very good opinion of me in the past."

She opened her mouth to defend herself, but words wouldn't form.

He grinned, his smile bewildering her senses even more. "No need to answer. Your silence says everything, and I won't pretend I don't deserve it."

His honest acknowledgement of his guilt surprised her. "Like I said, that was in the past."

He held up a hand. "No. You might accept that, but I don't. I'd like to start by apologizing, Afton. I was a complete and utter jerk to make love with you and then never call."

Were they really having this conversation? She could only blink and stare.

He studied her, his dark gaze penetrating hers, leaving her with goose bumps. "I know it's not a good excuse, but I was young and stupid and not smart enough to realize what I was doing. I was far too worried about my parents figuring out I'd been out all night. Instead, I should have been thinking about you."

She quickly waved his apology away as awkwardness crept over her. "There's nothing to forgive. It wasn't as though I didn't know your intentions when you led me away from the party to the secluded hillside behind the cabin."

He closed his eyes for a moment. "Still. Just know, it meant something to me despite my actions afterward. I remember parts of that night so clearly, like you commenting on the moon."

Memories tugged at her, and she appreciated knowing that his feelings and words that night had been genuine. "I remember, too. It was a huge super moon that lit up the entire sky."

"Yes." He held her gaze and smiled. "Afton, if you'll give me the chance, I'd like to change your mind about me and prove I'm a decent guy."

She widened her eyes, shocked at his admission and feeling trapped. "What do you mean?"

He took a step away from her, giving her space. "I have a couple of steaks chilling in the fridge, and I happen to be an excellent cook. If you'll allow me, I'd like to make dinner for you."

She struggled to find her mental footing. "You...want to cook...for me?"

"I do." He gave her a firm nod. "Very much so."

His invitation had taken her completely by surprise, and she couldn't begin to guess his motivation. Surely, it wasn't because she had a poor opinion of him. "Why?"

He shrugged. "Because I like you. And I'd like to catch up on what you've been doing since that summer when..." He finished with a devastating smile.

She lifted a brow, studying his expression, trying to decipher his intent.

Damn it all to hell. How could one smile from him steal any rational thoughts or reservations she might have? She'd need to be ever vigilant if she intended to resist him. "I hope you're not looking for a repeat performance."

Instead of being offended, he widened his smile. "I'd never be so arrogant as to assume that. To be honest, I'd really like to spend some time with the woman who talked so philosophically at seventeen and who also wasn't afraid to stand up to Mayor Gardiner. Few in town could claim the same. Perhaps I can learn something from you."

She searched his expression, looking for signs of insincerity, but she found none. "Really?"

He lifted his hand. "I'll swear on a bible if you'd like. It won't be the first time this week. Dinner and enlightening conversation. Nothing more. I promise I won't sleep with you, even if you beg."

An unexpected laugh spilled from her. "I bet you would. If I begged."

Laughter lit his dark eyes. "Okay. You win. I probably would. But you won't, so I can promise you're safe."

She shook her head in mock dismay. "I'm no longer sure what you're promising and what you're not."

"Perfect then. That's the sign of a good politician."

She studied him, trying to decide her best course of action. "How about if we promise to leave that night in the past? What's done is done."

He slowly shook his head. "I don't know. That was an amazing night."

She wanted to wrap her arms around his pretty words, but she didn't dare. She appreciated his apology, but that didn't erase what he'd done. "It's the only way I'll agree to stay."

"You drive a hard bargain. One I can't refuse." He held out an elbow for her. "Shall we move this party to the kitchen?"

7

Corey couldn't explain why he'd canceled dinner with Mallory and had invited Afton to stay, other than he knew he'd regret the second she walked out his front door. He was determined to prolong that moment for as long as possible.

With her fingers tucked around his arm, he led her deeper into the house, heady sensations detonating left and right inside him. His dad and Dwight would have a coronary if they discovered that the one woman they'd warned him against now stood in his kitchen. They'd call him rebellious. But he hadn't invited her to stay to prove he made his own choices. He didn't feel the need to prove that to anyone.

He'd invited her to stay because she was the one woman who hadn't been intimidated by his supposed status in town. She was the one who'd been his match in intelligence, even when she was seventeen. The one woman who'd made his blood pound hotter than Hades.

She was the one he'd never been able to forget, and he'd often wondered if she could have been *the one,* as crazy as that seemed.

Some might argue time had enhanced his memories of her, of

their night together. But one look at the lovely vision in front of him would prove them wrong. In the past and still today, he'd been told to steer clear of her, but he no longer allowed the fears of others to control him.

"Have a seat, and I'll pour you a glass of wine," he said, leaving her next to a bar stool. "Unless you'd prefer whiskey."

She hesitated, and he wondered if she'd caught his reference to their past. If so, she didn't let on. "Wine would be perfect."

He stood rooted, watching as she slid onto the stool, catching a whiff of her sexy scent. Then he rotated on his heels and strode to the pantry, trying to keep his wits. After looking inside, he glanced over his shoulder and caught her checking out his ass. "I have a decent merlot or a pinot noir. What sounds better?"

She widened her eyes as an attractive blush colored her cheeks. "Uh, how about the pinot?"

The slow burn of attraction lit deep inside him. "Perfect."

He stared at her for a few awkward seconds longer, unable to look away. Then he blinked and pulled a bottle from the rack. He snatched a corkscrew from a drawer and two long-stemmed glasses from the cupboard.

He set the bottle on the counter in front of her and prepared to uncork it. "I'm glad we ran into each other last night."

Her expression flashed with uncertainty. "I thought we were drinking the pinot?"

Perplexed, he glanced down at the bottle, unnerved to find his distraction had caused him to grab the wrong one. "Right."

He'd been too focused on the way her hair fell in a wave of blond silk over her shoulder. He shook his head and retrieved the correct bottle.

An entertained smile hovered on her lips when he returned. "Did you know if you put it in the freezer for fifteen minutes, it will enhance the flavors?"

He arched a brow at the new information. "Is that so?"

She lifted a shoulder and let it drop, but he could sense her amusement.

"That's what we'll do then. It can chill while I work on dinner." He made a show of taking the bottle to the freezer and placing it inside. "I hadn't realized you were a wine connoisseur in addition to whiskey."

She smiled, a tease shining from her eyes. "I actually drink wine more often than whiskey, but don't tell my grandpa. He'd be so disappointed."

Corey snorted a laugh. "Understandable, though I'll admit he's improved the taste of his whiskey over the years."

"He has. Some of his blends are amazing. And you would know this because..." She fingered the stem of her empty glass, distracting him again with a knowing smile.

His insides warmed. "Because I live in Aspen, and I drink whiskey from time to time."

"Gasp. You drink bootleg whiskey?" she said in a secretive whisper. "Do your constituents know?"

He couldn't keep the grin from his face. "Some of them. The ones who are truly my friends. The others don't need to know that much detail about my personal life. They just need to be assured I have their best interests at heart."

She studied his face, her gaze drifting to his lips before she dragged it upward. "Do you? Have their best interests at heart?"

Pride welled inside him. "I'd like to think so, yes." He half expected her to argue with him, but she only nodded.

"So, dinner," he said, changing the subject before continuing to flirt with her made him totally lose his head. "Steaks, maybe a salad?"

She nodded. "Can I help?"

"No, you cannot. You can sit there and keep me company while I handle it."

A wide smile brightened her face. She pulled her bottom lip

inward to hide her pleasure, but it was too late. He'd caught her expression and enjoyed the hell out of it. "Why the smile?"

"It's just..." Afton hesitated. "*You* are the first man *ever* to cook for me."

His gaze turned skeptical. "I don't believe it. What about your grandpa?"

She snorted. "If you can call that cooking. He might know how to brew a batch of whiskey, but he's a disaster in the kitchen. I'd been living with him and starving for nearly a week when I took over the duties."

He'd known she hadn't always lived in Aspen, but he couldn't remember the exact year she'd moved in. He pulled the salad contents from the fridge and began washing lettuce in the sink at the bar. As he worked, he continually glanced at her. "How old were you then?"

"Eight."

That was so young. He remembered she'd been nothing but a beanpole, but she'd always had that beautiful blond hair. "Your parents...died?" He said the last word cautiously, not wanting to resurrect painful memories.

She flicked her gaze to him, pinning him with eyes the color of lush summer grass. "Something like that."

Instinct warned him not to press, but he couldn't help wanting to know more about her. He turned off the water and set the lettuce aside before he picked up a succulent tomato. "So, not dead, then."

She exhaled and smiled. "Let's talk about something else."

He didn't like it when people pressed him about personal business, either. She'd tell him if and when she was ready. For now, he'd be happy to have her company. "Okay."

8

Afton relished the experience of Corey pampering her. He'd cooked her steak to perfection and kept her glass filled with lovely wine, though it left her tipsy. Even though the evening was mild, she sat on his secluded back patio, snuggled into a warm hoodie that smelled deliciously like him, the overhead light surrounding them in a soft glow.

His apology had paved the way for her to sit comfortably in his presence. He couldn't know how vulnerable she still was to his charms, but at least he wasn't the jerk she'd assumed he was.

Right now, he was handsome and attentive, providing her with a delightful evening. Much more than she'd ever expected from him.

A soft breeze rustled the leaves in the trees around the house. Beyond them, evergreen pines and aspens covered the land while shadowy figures rose into the hills as the sun escaped into the night.

She pointed off in the distance. "If I walked east, eventually, I'd run into my house. I think."

He turned in that direction and snorted. "Yeah, but I wouldn't advise it. There's a lot of rough terrain between here and there."

She leaned back in her chair and studied the curvature of his brow and the sensuous line of his lips. "Is this where you sat to paint your picture? I can't see if the little shack is visible because it's too dark now, but the view reminds me of your work."

His soft chuckle vibrated her senses. "I actually hiked into the hills, but, yes, the same general view."

She sighed, her whole body warm and relaxed. "You're a very talented man, Mr. Kendall. What else can you do?"

"Hmm...I don't know." He buried his grin behind a sip of wine. "You already know I'm a sly politician and an amazing architect. What about you?"

She thought for a moment. "I'm going to open a highly profitable whiskey distillery this year, and I'm a foster mom."

He leaned forward. "A foster mom, seriously?"

She enjoyed the surprised look on his face before she clarified. "For dogs," she said with a light-hearted laugh. "I helped over thirty dogs find homes in Denver, and now I'm doing the same in Aspen. Currently, I have a sweet golden retriever pup looking for a home. If you know anyone who might be interested..."

"That's impressive, Afton." He seemed sincere. "What a great way to give back to our community."

She shrugged, seeming nonchalant, but his approval left a warm glow burning inside her. "They give me more than I do them."

"I love dogs."

His intense stare sent flutters through her heart. "Really? That's great." She'd long since lost herself in his gaze, making it difficult to find more words.

"That's going to be a hard one to top." He lifted his glass and sipped. "Wait. I know. I can dance."

"Can you now?" His admission brought a vivid image to mind, one of him holding her in his arms, moving her body to sultry music. Except *she* couldn't dance. "You have me on that one. Sadly, I regret that I never learned how to dance very well."

He chuckled. "You did just fine that night by the campfire. If I remember correctly, you had some damn sexy moves."

She snorted and rolled her eyes. "First of all, I was drunk. Second, you were flat out wasted and in no shape to judge my dance moves."

"You were only tipsy when we..." He lifted his brows instead of finishing his sentence.

"I thought we agreed to leave that night in the past." She said it as a tease, but it reminded her of painful times she preferred to leave behind.

"Right. I did promise."

He nodded thoughtfully, and she could only guess what he might be thinking.

Corey sat forward and placed his glass on the table between them. Then he stood and held out his hand to her with a flourish. "Tonight is the night to erase our regrets. I've spoken my peace, and you want to perfect your dancing skills."

Sudden alarm spiked inside her, and she glanced with unease at the hand he held out to her. "What? You mean right now?"

His eyes sparked with mischief, tempting her. "We only have this moment, Afton. No guarantees we'll have tomorrow."

She could see why so many in Aspen supported him. With that smile and those eyes, it was hard not to want to put her fate in his hands.

The alarms going off in her head stemmed from the fear created in the past. She was a woman now, aware of the consequences that came with her choices. She could resist him if he tried anything more than dancing.

Afton set her glass next to his and stood, slipping her hand into his. He wrapped warm fingers around hers, and she fought to inhale a regular breath. The world spun at a faster rate. She'd like to blame it all on the wine, but she'd considerably slowed her drinking, knowing she'd need to drive home before long.

He moved to an open space on the slate patio and put her free hand high on his shoulder before he placed his on her back. Although his shirt stood between his skin and her fingertips, she enjoyed the curve of his powerful muscles resting beneath her touch.

"Keep your stance solid." He tugged on her arm, forcing her to provide resistance. "Not stiff, though."

She tried to relax while keeping her arm muscles taut.

"You need them tight in order to receive my cues."

"Okay." She wondered how she'd be able to focus on his instructions with him so close.

He grinned at her, obviously enjoying their play. "Let's see. We could waltz or swing."

She tried to remember the last time she'd truly enjoyed herself, like she was with him. "Could we start with the cha-cha? I sort of remember the basic steps."

He tilted his head in consent. "Of course. Nothing like a sexy Latin dance."

Her pulse fluttered from his nearness. She could see each individual lash framing his dark, sexy eyes, the singular threads in his shirt, and the fresh stubble from each of his whiskers. "Only if you're sure."

"Oh, I'm sure, Afton. Let's see what you remember." He started with one foot slightly back from the other, and she followed suit. "Ready?"

She laughed, her nerves chattering inside her. "No, but I have a feeling you'll make me dance, anyway."

Amused confidence shone in his expression. "And you'd be right."

He counted out the beats as he moved her backward and forward, and she found her body remembered the dance better than she would have believed. She rocked her hips and concentrated on keeping her movements loose and sensual.

He looked down at her and grinned. "I thought you didn't know how to dance."

His comment stole her attention, and she lost her rhythm. She stepped forward when she shouldn't have, and her shoe landed on his. She glanced down at their feet, embarrassed at her clumsiness. "*Oh, no.*"

He tilted her face up with a finger. "You didn't hurt me, Afton. Don't worry about it. People don't get this close without bumping into each other from time to time."

She rolled her eyes.

He chuckled. "I mean it. You're doing great. Let's try it with music."

Corey pulled the phone from his pocket, and soon a lively Latin song echoed into the night. She tugged his hoodie over her head and tossed it aside, now warm from exertion.

He absentmindedly set his phone on the table, all his attention on her.

A deep shiver expanded from her core as he sauntered back to her, his gaze racing over her while she made the same assessments of him.

He was tall with a trim waist and nice muscles. Much more a man than the boy she'd known. His dark hair and dark eyes spoke of hushed danger, and, Lord help her, appealed to each of her overactive senses.

The rational part of her knew intuitively she'd jumped into something deep, and it begged her to run while she could.

Instead, she waited for him, anticipating his touch once again. Regardless of how strongly her conscience urged her to walk away, she couldn't. Her wild and spontaneous side embraced the delightful sensations he created, and she just wanted the tiniest taste. She'd be fine.

Corey held out his arms, and she stepped into them without thinking twice. One thing Grandpa had always taught her was to live for the moment, because it might be all she had. She'd been burned before, most notably by the man who held her, but she'd also learned not to dwell on the past and keep her focus on the future.

Neither of them were the people they used to be, which left the future exciting and uncertain. She'd experienced a connection to him their first night together. Later, she'd written it off as a foolish fantasy. Now, she wondered again.

"Ready?" he asked, pleasure radiating from his eyes. He'd spoken of dancing, but her mind immediately questioned if she was ready for whatever lay hidden beyond the current moment.

"I think so." Despite her ineptitude, she cherished the moments of innocent play and flirtation. Her secret attraction to him thrilled her. And for a few moments, she dreamed about what her future might be if he felt the same.

He held her, staring into her eyes as he waited for the appropriate beat to start. She couldn't help her smile, and when he returned it, he stoked the fire inside her. He began to move, and she held his gaze. The music made her movements more instinctual, and she lost herself in his mesmerizing eyes.

"Good," he murmured, his smile radiating his approval. "You're a better dancer than you know."

She shook her head in disagreement but basked in his compliment. "Only because you know what you're doing."

"I disagree." He stopped and turned her, catching her off guard, but she quickly caught the beat again. "Not everyone has your natural instinct."

She laughed. "If I followed my better instincts, I wouldn't be dancing with you."

He tilted his head, seeming genuinely perplexed by her statement. "Why not?"

"Because we're on opposite sides of an issue. Because my grandpa and your daddy don't like each other very much. Because we're two people who were never meant to be together and should have learned our lesson the first time." There. She'd spoken her fears.

Instead of growing sad or angry, he laughed. "It's just a dance, Afton."

"Is it?" she countered.

The strong currents of attraction weren't flowing in only one direction. Otherwise, they wouldn't be so powerful. "If I walk away, and we never speak again outside Town Hall, would you be okay with that?"

He stared at her for a long moment as they continued to dance. Then suddenly he stopped, his gaze dark with intent. "No."

His response shot a swift shiver through her, stealing her breath. Memories of identical feelings from six years ago jumped to life, overwhelming her. She forced a laugh, attempting to diffuse the situation long enough to allow her to gain her bearings. "Told you so."

9

Afton's beautiful green eyes fascinated the hell out of Corey. So pretty. So intriguing. Just like the rest of her, including the wheels in her mind that constantly turned. Her question about how he'd react if she walked away had caught him off-guard, forcing him to examine their situation. But he loved she wasn't afraid to call things as she saw them.

However, he did fear that she might walk out of his life like she'd suggested without giving him a chance to explore his inexplicable attraction to her. He met her gaze, hers a challenging flash of enticement and determination. "You make it sound like we're on two opposing sides that could never find middle ground."

She shrugged and returned to the table to pick up her glass of wine. "It seems that way from my perspective."

He followed her and allowed her to take a sip before he took the glass from her and set it down. She watched his movements but didn't say anything. He enjoyed her small but sharp intake of breath when he cupped her chin between his forefinger and thumb. Interest flared in her eyes, heating his blood.

Her lips caught his attention for a moment, and he sensed her respiration had increased along with his. Then he blinked and focused on her eyes. "Here's how it is. I decide whose side I'm on and whose company I'd like to keep. Just me. I don't care what my father, your grandfather, or anyone else thinks."

She wetted her bottom lip with her tongue before she spoke. "And I say you're more influenced by your daddy than you're willing to admit. What would he say if he walked out right now and found us like this?"

Like this? Like what, he wanted to question, but her mouth had stolen his attention once again, and really, all he wanted to know in that moment was one thing. "Do you still taste like strawberries?"

Confusion colored her expression. "Do I... Strawberries?"

"I don't care what anyone thinks, Afton. I just want to know if you still taste like strawberries." Before she could respond, he threaded his fingers through the silky strands at the base of her neck and lowered his lips to hers.

She released the most sensual sigh when their mouths met, making him instantly hard.

He wrapped his free hand around her waist and tugged her against him, needing to feel more of her.

"Mmm..." he moaned, recognizing the sweet taste of strawberries on her lips. When he tried to deepen their kiss, she pulled back with a laugh.

"Oh, my God." She placed her fingers over her lips.

He tightened his grip on her, unwilling to lose this moment so quickly. "What?"

"That was a bold move." Her voice held a chuckle, her expression amused.

"Maybe so, but I've been known to go after what I want."

She snorted and looked away before she turned her beautiful eyes on him once again. "I seem to recall you saying something similar all those years ago."

"Yeah? Could be." He'd never had a problem knowing what he wanted and going for it. At least not until he met Afton. "I guess some things never change."

She searched his gaze, her expression full of flirtation and a touch of hesitation. "And yet some things do."

He exhaled, wishing his erection would let some blood return to his brain so he could decipher her meaning. When that didn't seem a possibility, he cradled her face between his hands, prepared to steal another kiss.

He enjoyed a delicious moment of his mouth against hers before the sound of his doorbell chime broke their kiss.

"Who the hell would that be this late at night?"

Afton shrugged and stepped away as though they'd been caught doing something they shouldn't. That bothered him.

He picked up his phone and paused the music. "Stay here. I'll be right back." He cursed under his breath as he headed into the house, prepared to send away whoever was on the other side of his door.

———

Evening sounds kept Afton company as the night air cooled her heated skin. Corey had left the back door ajar in his rush to get inside, leaving the interior lights to spill out and mingle with the patio lighting.

Feeling awkward, she moved to the table and sat, the chilled cushion cool against her jeans. She lifted her glass to sip, but paused as a female voice echoed through the house.

"I hope you don't mind that I stopped by. After canceling our date earlier, I knew you'd be working hard and would probably forget to eat. So, I brought some of my famous baked chicken with your favorite mashed potatoes."

Afton stiffened and quietly set her glass on the patio table.

Was this woman his girlfriend? He'd obviously had a date with her, and she seemed to know him well enough to think it would be okay for her to bring over food.

She swallowed the sickening lump of bile that rose in her throat, along with a healthy dose of humiliation. She hadn't heard any rumors that Corey was seriously attached, but she hadn't been back in town for very long, and she'd had no reason to ask anyone about him.

God, this was exactly like six years ago, when she'd learned, after sleeping with him, he'd officially started dating Emily Clinton only a month prior. Were the fates loading up the same scenario to see if she'd learned any life lessons the first go round?

If so, they'd be happy to know she sure as hell had.

She mentally kicked herself for falling for his undeniable charms once again. He was smooth. She'd give him that. Feeding her, plying her with wine and sweet words. She couldn't say for certain she wouldn't have ended up in his bed that night, but she'd like to think she would have declined.

She picked up her purse and headed around the side of the house toward her car parked along the darkened street. She'd considered walking in the back door just to see the shock on the woman's face and to let Corey know he wasn't as sly as he'd like to think.

But the effort wasn't worth the small amount of satisfaction she'd gain. Plus, it wouldn't help matters if she angered him. He had the power, along with the other council members, to grant or deny her a business license.

She had her grandpa's dream to save, a damn petition to fill, and that's where she'd focus her energy. The only thing she needed from Corey was his vote.

———

It was after nine in the evening when she parked in front of her house. She was surprised to find Joanna Ewing's gold Corolla there as well. She couldn't imagine what her best friend's mom, who also happened to be a nurse, might be doing there so late at night. Unless...

No.

Afton exited her car, rushed across the gravel drive, and let herself into the house, hoping her grandfather hadn't had trouble with his asthma again. The lights were out except in the kitchen, and she could hear them in there talking.

Grandpa's laugh boomed as she reached the doorway, sending a flood of relief through her. He was fine. Joanna had stopped by for a friendly visit, not for anything medically related.

They sat at the nicked wooden table, a pitcher of clear liquid between them, both with half-filled glasses in their hands.

"Afton," her grandpa announced when he noticed her, seeming uncomfortable that she'd intruded.

"Hey, Grandpa." She eyed her best friend's mom, who still had her dark hair pulled back and wore nursing scrubs. She must have stopped in on her way home from work. "Hi, Joanna. How are things at the medical center? Enjoying the new addition?"

Her dark eyes flashed. "Work is work. As for having an updated environment, too many things need to be adjusted. I'm getting too old for such nonsense. I just want to do my job and go home."

Afton nodded, trying to decipher their awkwardness. "What are you all drinking? It looks like water, but Grandpa never drinks it straight without something to sweeten it."

Joanna smiled. "Yep. Just water. Your grandpa tried to give me coffee, but if I drink it this late at night, I'll never get to sleep."

Grandpa's eyes lit as he watched her speak. "I offered the lady whiskey, too, but she declined. Said I made her tipsy."

Afton blinked in surprise. He *was flirting* with her.

The woman's cheeks colored. "I said *your whiskey* makes me tipsy, and I need to drive home tonight."

He tilted his head, his salt and pepper mustache turning up as he grinned. "No one said you have to go home tonight. You know you're always welcome to stay here," he said, his accent more prominent than usual.

Afton fought to keep from snorting. Never in her life had she witnessed him be such a flirt. "Grandpa."

"What?" He shrugged. "Just being neighborly."

Joanna stood. "I should head home, anyway. Good to see you, missy. I know your grandpa is happy to have you here."

"You, too. Tell Laurel I said hi when you talk to her, and that I'll call her soon. We've both been so busy that we kind of lost touch. Oh! Wait."

The sight of her grandpa with another woman had caused her temporarily to forget her current purpose in life. "How would you feel about signing a petition to support our new business efforts?"

Joanna waved her hand. "Oh, honey, you know you both always have my support. Do you have the petition with you?"

Afton pointed toward the front of the house. "It's in my car. Let me get it."

"That would be wonderful. Better yet, why don't you hold off and meet me and Laurel at Rumors on Saturday morning at nine for breakfast? It's my day off, and I know she'd love to see you. We can both sign then, and you might gather a few more signatures while we're there."

Afton's heart warmed with thoughts of her old friend. "Laurel's in town? I thought she wouldn't be back until the fall."

"Yep. She's been back for a few weeks. All finished with college, just like you."

Breakfast sounded perfect. "*Of course*, I'll be there. I can't wait to see her." She hugged her so-called surrogate mother goodbye as Grandpa gave his *friend* a not-so-cryptic see you later. Joanna picked up her bag from the floor and headed out.

Afton waited until their friend had left the house before she took a seat at the table across from her grandfather.

He looked up at her from beneath bushy brows. "What?"

"Is there something going on I should know about?" she asked in the most serious tone she could muster.

He widened his eyes and leaned back in his chair, looking guiltier than sin. "What do you mean?"

"I'm wondering why Joanna would pay a visit this late at night, not to mention both of you looked pretty guilty when I walked in."

"We didn't look guilty," he tossed back to her with a rush of words. "There's nothing to look guilty for. She just stops in from time to time."

Afton raised her brows, hoping to squeeze out a confession.

"For whiskey, Afton. She likes my new malt blend."

She sent him an unconvinced look. "Uh-huh. Okay." If he didn't want to spill yet, that was fine. But she knew one thing for damn sure.

Joanna hadn't walked out with any whiskey bottles.

He glanced at his watch. "Which reminds me, where have you been? I thought you had a quick errand."

"I did. It took me longer than I expected."

"Where did you go?" he prodded.

She thought about lying, but she, in contrast to him, had nothing to hide. "I stopped by Councilmember Kendall's office." House. Whatever.

He narrowed his eyes. "Why?"

"To see if he could do anything to help our petition." No guilt. No shame.

He exhaled a deep breath. "Number one, I already told you I don't want to push it that far. Number two, I don't like you around that man. Any of those bastards, to be exact. I think we need to stop this whole thing right now."

She pulled the water pitcher and Joanna's glass closer to her, preparing to take them to the sink. "I didn't push anything. It was a simple request."

"What did he say?"

She forced a smile. "He said there wasn't much he could do until we had the signatures."

He tipped his head in an I-told-you-so look. "See?"

She continued, as though she hadn't heard his last comment. "But he also gave me the name of a woman who could help rally interest if we have a problem getting signatures."

He shook his head in warning.

"I'm not pushing anything," she repeated. "You said you were fine with the petition. That's all I'm doing."

He released another, less forceful sigh. "Fine. But stay away from Kendall."

She narrowed her gaze at his request. "What do you have against Corey? Other than who his father is?"

Her grandfather pinned her with a piercing look. "That's enough of a black mark right there. But more, I don't like the way he looks at you."

"What do you mean, the way he looks at me? He doesn't look at me in any particular way." Well, aside from their time several years ago and maybe for a few minutes that evening in his backyard.

"He looks at you like he wants to..." He nodded several times as though that was an effective means of communication.

Which she supposed it was because she knew exactly what he meant. "That's your overactive imagination, Grandpa."

"Bullshit. A guy knows exactly what another guy is thinking when he looks at a woman like that."

She wasn't about to have this discussion with her grandfather. "Really? Would that be how you were looking at Joanna when I walked in?"

He stood, his chair scraping the worn wooden laminate. He gathered his glass, plus the other dishes Afton had in front of her. "Don't get sassy with me, young lady. I know what I saw, and don't you doubt it. Stay away from the Kendalls. They're as bad as Gardiner, and they'll bring nothing but trouble."

Afton followed her grandpa to the sink and gave him a kiss on his lined cheek. "You have nothing to worry about. I have no intention of going anywhere near Corey Kendall again. I'm too smart for that."

10

Afton arrived at Rumors Coffee Shop a few minutes after nine on Saturday. As she pushed through the front entrance into the cheerful café, Laurel jumped from her seat and rushed toward her with a squeal.

"Oh, my God, Afton. You look so good," Laurel said as she pulled away.

"Me? Look at you. Since when do you wear your hair red?"

"I'm thinking about keeping it this color. What do you think?" Laurel slid her fingers through the long length of straight hair.

"It's gorgeous. *You're* gorgeous." Time had definitely been kind to her friend.

Laurel laughed. "I decided I needed to put away my boots from time to time and start acting like a lady if I wanted to attract a man."

Afton snorted. "Whatever. You were pretty before."

"Maybe so." Laurel linked her arm through Afton's as they walked toward the table where she'd been sitting. "Problem is, the guys don't take the time to stop and look when my hair is stuffed into a hat."

Afton laughed as she took the seat across from Laurel. "Silly boys."

"Right?" Laurel pushed an empty coffee cup and a carafe toward Afton. "I ordered a pot for us, and April's bringing her heavenly cinnamon rolls as soon as she frosts them."

Only two cups sat on the table. "Where's your mom?"

"She'll be late, which is good. We need some alone time to catch up, don't you think? Can't quite talk about everything with her here. Not that I don't love her, but you know..."

"I understand. No matter how old I get, I'm still not talking sex with my grandpa. Not that I need to worry. He'd never try. He couldn't say the word last night when he warned me away from Corey Kendall."

Laurel's eyes brightened. "Why would he be worried about Corey? I thought he and Mallory O'Brien were an item."

Too bad she didn't know that before she'd gone to Corey's house. She could have spared herself some embarrassment. "Either way, my grandpa has no reason to worry about him."

Afton imparted brief details over what had transpired the past two days, but stalled when she reached the part where Corey had invited her to stay for dinner. She wasn't sure why she'd mentioned him in the first place, since everything that had happened the previous evening meant nothing.

Laurel gave her an encouraging nod. "And..."

"Why does there have to be an *and*?" Afton lifted her cup and sipped, using the hot coffee as an excuse not to meet her friend's gaze.

"Uh-uh. Don't sit there and try to hide anything from me. I can see right through you."

She grinned, realizing how much she'd missed this kind of interaction with her friend. "No, you can't."

"Oh, yes, I can. I've always been able to."

Afton studied Laurel and smiled. "I call bullshit." Not once had her friend caught a drift of what had happened that fateful summer.

"Call it all you want, but I'm right. And don't think I don't know what you're thinking right now, because I do. I can see it in your eyes. You might not have talked much about that night with Corey years ago, but that doesn't mean it went unnoticed."

"What night?" Afton lifted a shoulder and let it drop as though she had no clue, but her insides twisted. She and Laurel had always been close, but there was no way the woman could read her mind.

"Really?" Laurel leaned forward as her coffee-colored eyes sparkled with mischief. "How about a certain Saturday night in June, not long after graduation, when you were seen dancing with Corey, and then disappeared afterward?"

Afton slumped in her chair, a frown forcing its way onto her lips. "Why didn't you ever say anything?"

"I didn't know what to say. I thought about questioning you, but you were so sad after that night. For a long time afterward, too. I didn't want to make things worse." She leaned in closer. "Did he force himself on you?" she asked in a whisper.

"What?" Afton straightened. "No. Why would you ask that?"

Laurel shrugged. "You were so fragile afterward and kind of withdrawn. Then we both went away to school, and you seemed fine in your emails, so I didn't know what to think."

"Wow, Laurel. I wasn't raped, okay? I hate thinking that's what you've been wondering all these years." It was worse than the actual truth. "Did you say that to anyone else?"

Laurel shook her head. "No. I would never talk about you like that. You know you can trust me."

Apparently, life would not let her leave all those miserable, ugly feelings in the past. Instead, they popped up like caskets during a flood. "He didn't rape me...but I did sleep with him."

She pointed at Afton. "I knew it."

Afton narrowed her gaze in annoyance.

Laurel chuckled. "Come on. You can't be mad at me. I'm the one who's been slighted. *You slept with Corey?* You'd lusted after him our entire senior year, finally slept with him, and you never said anything to me, *your best friend?*" Laurel folded her arms and leaned back in her chair. "I'm not sure I can talk to you right now."

The humor of the situation finally hit her. "I'm sorry—"

"No." Laurel held up a hand and turned her head, giving her a healthy dose of mock injury. "It's too late."

"Laurel." Afton reached out and covered her friend's hand. "Forgive me. Besides, I know you well enough to know you can't hold a grudge longer than five minutes. So, no matter what, in five minutes, we'll be friends again. You might as well give it up now."

Laurel slid a glance toward her, held it for a few seconds, and then smiled. "I hate it when you're right."

Afton grinned and shook her head. "This is why I love you."

"Yeah, I know. Oh, look. April has our delicious reason to live."

"Morning, ladies." April's brunette ponytail swung over her shoulder as she set a huge cinnamon roll between them before passing out two forks. "Enjoy that."

"You're truly an evil being," Afton said with a laugh. "If I don't die from pleasure, I'll surely die from an overload of calories."

"Neither one sounds like a bad way to go, if you ask me." April winked and headed back to work.

"I'm in love with her," Laurel said as she forked a bite of cinnamon roll. "Or at least with her cooking. Seth Moore is a lucky man."

"Agreed. How come when a couple hooks up, guys get the better end of the deal? Maybe we women would like a housewife to come home to, someone who will cook or clean for us."

"No kidding," Laurel said around a mouthful. "Though some guys will do that."

"Not many that I know." Except Corey *had* cooked for her, had even insisted she couldn't help. "Really, what do women get out of the arrangement besides someone to take care of?"

Laurel raised a perfectly plucked eyebrow in a hopeful gesture. "Good sex and someone to lift heavy things?"

Afton sighed in defeat. "You're right. There is that. I guess we can't totally discount those benefits."

"Nope." Laurel chased her bite with a drink of coffee. "So, back to our original conversation. What's up with you and Corey?"

She snorted. "There's nothing up with him. What's past is past, and you sound like my grandpa."

"Uh-huh." Laurel narrowed her eyes, but Joanna's arrival spared Afton from further questioning.

"Hey, Mom." Laurel stood and hugged her mother, and Afton did the same.

"Did you bring your petition, missy?" the older woman asked Afton.

Afton resumed her seat, retrieved a clipboard with several attached papers, and proudly passed it to Joanna. "Thank you so much for your support. It means everything."

She signed her name with a flourish and handed the petition to Laurel. "Happy to do it."

Laurel snatched her mom's pen. "You know what you should do? Go stand on the corner near Randall's Outfitters and catch people as they walk down the street. I bet you'd get a ton of signatures that way. I could do the same outside Anderson's Grocery. They're the busiest places in town."

"That's not a bad idea," Afton said.

Joanna stole Laurel's fork from her fingers and cut a bite of cinnamon roll. "Not to be a wet towel, but I think your grandpa is torn over this whole thing. He didn't seem too certain last night that he wanted to pursue it any longer."

Afton blew out a frustrated breath. "He was a month ago and a week ago. I don't know why he suddenly has cold feet."

"I agree," Laurel said. "Your grandpa was always the first to stand up to bullies. Is he feeling okay?"

"I think so. He hasn't said anything." She searched her memory for clues but came up blank. "Other than this odd character behavior, he seems like his usual feisty self." She glanced at Joanna.

"He is getting older," she replied with a shrug. "Maybe he'd rather focus on something else."

"I know," Laurel said. "Maybe he's decided he doesn't want the attention. Everyone in town is talking about what went down at the meeting, and you know he likes his privacy."

"That is so true," Afton said. "He'll always stick up for others, but he doesn't like it when the focus is on him. Still, he's wanted this distillery for a long time."

A sparkle lit in Laurel's eyes. "Maybe he's hiding something like a lurid past. And he's worried someone will figure him out. He does have that mysterious, bad-ass persona even at his age."

Afton laughed.

Joanna gave Laurel a pointed look. "Or maybe someone likes to embellish, making up ridiculous, sensational stories to get a reaction."

"Why do you think I went into journalism?" Laurel tossed back with a smile.

Joanna shook her head before turning to Afton. "I'm sure he's fine, honey. Maybe he's had time to think about things and has realized having a legitimate brand is not worth the energy it will cost him after all."

Afton sighed. "Maybe so."

However, her grandpa's attitude still didn't sit right with her. He'd never backed down from a fight. Especially not one that involved something he was passionate about.

Something was off with him, and a burning need to discover what exactly that was wouldn't leave her alone. The first thing she would do after spending a morning collecting signatures would be to pin him down. "Perhaps if I reassure him that I'll do all the legwork, he'll feel better."

"Don't forget you also have help," Laurel said. "Neither one of you is in this alone. If you have an extra clipboard in that bag of yours, we should get started on the petitions as soon as we're done here. We could catch the Saturday morning traffic through town. If your grandpa changes his mind down the road, no problem. We'll toss them. But it's going to take a while to catch a hundred people when they're out and about, which is still going to be easier than going door to door."

Afton thought for a moment, excitement surging inside her. The energy put toward this project didn't have to come from her grandfather. She could do it. Laurel would help. "Agreed. There's nothing that says we must submit the petition. Let's take the first step and worry about the rest later."

11

fton stood on the sidewalk near Randall's Western Outfitters. The bright morning sun warmed her, and a soft spring breeze drew her hair across her cheek.

Before she'd started, she'd gone home for a quick minute to pick up Sonny, worried he'd been home alone too long since Grandpa was in Pinecone for the morning. In hindsight, bringing him along had been a great idea. Several people had stopped to see the cute puppy and had ended up signing her petition.

Sonny ran a circle around her feet, tangling his leash about her legs as she counted the signatures she'd gathered. Eighteen. Not bad for a morning's work. Many people in Aspen woke early, tended to their business in town, and headed home for Saturday afternoon chores. In hindsight, she wished she hadn't spent an hour inside Rumors earlier, chatting away while she could have been gaining more signatures.

She would return later that night to catch the evening crowd who'd be going out for dinner or drinking at Sparrow's on a Saturday night. Plus, she could still contact the woman Corey had suggested. The stubborn, prideful part of her wanted to ignore the help he'd offered, but her rational side reminded her that the best form of revenge was success.

If she filled her petition, she'd force the council to reconsider their appeal. If enough people spoke on their behalf, she might push this through for her grandpa's sake.

That would really spark talk in her town.

Afton turned at the sound of a car door shutting behind her, prepared to approach her next potential supporter. The sight of Corey walking toward her flipped her stomach.

Oh, hell no.

She rotated on her heels and strode in the opposite direction, with Sonny releasing cute puppy barks at the newcomer. She had nothing to say to the man. Nothing nice, anyway. She'd meet up with Laurel instead.

"*Afton,*" Corey called after her.

He tried twice more before she stopped with a groan. "Just go away," she whispered.

Slow, steady breaths, she reminded herself. *Keep it professional. Remember he had a say in her future.* She swiveled when his footsteps sounded close. "Something I can help you with, Councilmember?"

Sonny furiously sniffed Corey's legs.

"I'm sorry." He took her hand before she could react. Genuine remorse darkened his beautiful eyes, leaving a worried expression on his face. "I put you in an awkward position last night, and I couldn't feel worse about it. I had no idea Mallory would show and bring dinner. I had canceled with her, and I think she was just trying to be nice."

She would make certain he wouldn't have a chance to place her in a similar situation in the future. Afton slid her hand from his. "Don't worry about it. I hope my presence didn't cause you or her any distress."

"Distress?" He tilted his head. "Why would you have?"

She snorted, amazed at his gall. Did he believe her still to be that naïve? "I'm certain your girlfriend wouldn't have been happy to find us dancing together on the patio."

At her comment, he smiled, his eyes lighting up. "First, Mallory isn't my girlfriend. We've dated a couple of times, but that's it. Second, I loved dancing with you and couldn't care less who knows about it."

He bent and scooped up Sonny, who was happy to smell and lick Corey's face. "I was extremely sad to find you'd left so quickly. Mallory wasn't there longer than five minutes, which was five minutes longer than I'd hoped to leave you waiting."

She studied him and the way he interacted with Sonny, who didn't seem to have any problems with the man. Corey seemed sincere, but she'd learned she couldn't always trust her instincts. "Well, I'm not the type to stand in the shadow of another woman. If she's bringing you food, she obviously believes there's more to your relationship, so..."

She pulled Sonny from his arms and set him on the ground before she took a step backward.

He erased the newly expanded distance between them. "Afton, she and I have no relationship. We dated. Twice."

"Regardless, appearances are important." So was protecting her heart. "As a politician, you should understand public perception better than anyone. People in Aspen believe you're a couple." And she wouldn't give the town a reason to suggest she might be the other woman.

One side of his mouth lifted in a mischievous grin that made her uncomfortable. "Is that so? What are they saying?"

She took another step back, his reaction leaving her unbalanced. "That they've seen you together. They thought you were a couple."

He advanced and took her hand, sending shivers through her. "These people you're quoting, have they seen us hold hands?"

She fought to shore up her defenses, but his touch left her vulnerable. Open to pain. "I don't know. They didn't mention it."

His gaze dropped to her mouth for a moment. "How about kissing? Have they witnessed me kissing her?"

A dark thrill raced through her, even as a small voice prompted her to run. "I didn't ask."

His smile widened. "But you would have to agree that if I *had* a girlfriend, it would be a damning move to kiss another woman in a public place. Say on the streets of downtown Aspen, with public perception being what it is."

She inhaled, prepared to voice an objection, but he tugged her against him. She placed a hand on his chest in a feeble gesture of resistance. "Corey..."

He gave her two seconds to escape, but she couldn't do it. He knew it. Knew he had her. Knew she could have pulled away and didn't.

He lowered his face toward hers and captured her mouth with a heated kiss that seared her soul. Sonny whined at their feet, but the feel of Corey's lips on hers stole her attention.

Oh, hell. The sentiment filtered through her mind before it dissolved into a thoughtless vapor that floated away on the warm breeze. *Delicious* filled the empty void. She placed a hand on his cheek, and he wrapped a possessive arm around her waist, molding her to him.

She fit his body perfectly.

His tongue tickled her bottom lip, and she opened her mouth without thinking. *She wanted him.* Against her better judgment. Wanted to taste him, to feel his wonderfully hard body against hers once again.

She remembered that night years ago when they'd been skin against skin. She'd relived it over and over in her memory so many times through the years when lonely nights had haunted her with unbearably quiet darkness.

She'd thought she'd had those feelings contained. She could allow them out when she'd wanted the experience, but she'd been able to secure the lid when it came time to put them away.

Until he'd kissed her the previous evening. That act seemed to have unleashed something uncontrollable inside her.

Sonny released a loud yip, jerking her back to reality.

She pushed against his chest, forcing him away. They stared at each other, their breaths coming at a faster pace, her pulse hot and racing. The intensity of her feelings for him frightened her. "This can't happen. Not again."

Worse, what if someone had seen them? What if they told her grandfather? What if the mayor found out? What if that scorching, sexy kiss somehow ruined her grandfather's chance of obtaining his business license?

What if she fell for him, only to have him break her heart again?

Without another word, she turned and hurried down the sidewalk toward Laurel. When he called her name again, Afton broke into a run, feeling as though the very devil chased at her heels along with Sonny.

She didn't stop until she reached Laurel, who stood near the front doors of Andersen's Grocery. Laurel held a cute baby girl while Katy Beckstead signed the petition.

Afton hung back, her breaths coming in winded pants. Sonny plopped at her feet and did the same. She glanced over her shoulder to ensure Corey had not followed.

He hadn't, thank God. After that devastating kiss, which she'd be lucky if no one had witnessed, the last thing she needed was for the townspeople to see him chasing her down the street. Already, events had the potential for disaster.

"There you go." Katy straightened, tucking her blond hair behind her ears as she held out the clipboard.

Laurel made the switch between the bundled baby and the clipboard. "Thank you."

Afton stepped forward. She'd never known Katy very well. With a few years between them and Katy coming from a much different background, they'd had few opportunities to interact. "Yes, thank you. My grandpa and I truly appreciate it."

Katy smiled. "Afton Searle, right?"

Afton returned the gesture. "Yes, and you're Katy Beckstead. Your wedding was absolutely beautiful. I loved the flowers."

"You were there?" She snorted and shook her head. "I'm so sorry. That was such a crazy, wonderful day, and I had a hard time keeping everyone straight."

Laurel and Afton both laughed.

"I'm sure you did," Afton said. "Besides, with a handsome guy like Scott, who would want to look at the guests? I came with my grandfather, Johnny Searle. Older guy with his hair in a pony-tail, and he likes to wear a bolero instead of a tie. He knows Scott."

Katy's lips parted in a warm grin. "I do remember him *and* you, now that you mention him. In fact, I'm certain Scott still has a bottle or two of your grandfather's whiskey in the basement. He says Sagecreek Whiskey is the best."

Happiness and pride filled Afton. Although her grandpa oper-ated behind the scenes, she couldn't help but be proud of what he'd accomplished. Creating fine whiskey was his passion, and it seemed so unfair that he had to keep to the shadows. Especially in this day and age. "Thank you for saying that. I'll be sure to tell him. And thank you again for signing. Your support means everything."

Katy shifted the baby in her arms. "No problem. I'm sure Scott would be happy to, as well."

Afton nodded toward Katy's daughter. "She's adorable."

"Isn't she?" Laurel agreed.

Katy laughed. "Thank you. She's a good baby. Hardly fusses at all."

The tiny infant focused on Laurel before a smile broke out on her lips.

"Oh! Look at that." Katy put her thumb next to her baby's hand, letting her grip it. "I think she likes you."

"Or it's gas," Laurel said, making them all laugh.

"Could be," Katy agreed. "I was actually thinking *your* baby was adorable, too, Afton."

She lifted Sonny from the ground. He wagged his tail and glanced from face to face, happy to be up where the action was. "He is, isn't he? But he's not permanently mine. I'm fostering him until we can find him a good home."

Katy ruffled his soft ears. "I can't believe how cute you are. Golden Retriever, right?"

"Yes," Afton replied, sensing genuine interest. "They're super friendly and great family dogs."

She smoothed her hand over his soft body, making Sonny far too excited. "I would really love to take him home, but I should probably check with my husband first."

"They do have a lot of energy and need to run," Afton cautioned.

"That wouldn't be a problem for us. We have a big yard that we've recently fenced, so when this little one gets older, she'll be safe." Katy shifted her gaze from the puppy to Afton. "If I'm interested, how do I go about adopting him?"

Excitement lit inside Afton. "Seriously? That would be so wonderful. He's a good boy with a sweet, sweet soul." She tore off a small corner of the petition and wrote her number. "I'll facilitate everything with the shelter in Pinecone."

"Thank you. I would really appreciate that. I'll let you know soon, in case you come across anyone else who might be interested." She left with a smile and a wave.

"I really like her," Laurel said as she turned to Afton. "I have sixteen signatures so far. You?"

"Eighteen. That's thirty-four in one morning. A third of what we'll need."

"Sweet." Laurel grinned. "Let's go to Sparrow's tonight."

Afton laughed. "I'd already planned on it. Thanks, Laurel. I really appreciate your help, and I'm starting to believe this is going to happen."

"Of course it is."

Afton fought to breathe a sigh of relief, but errant thoughts of Corey jumped in. Somewhere, out of her line of sight, was a singularly sexy man, who'd placed a burning kiss on her lips only moments before, who, she also knew, would not leave things as they were.

Someone had lit a fire beneath a pot of trouble, and it was only beginning to boil.

12

Afton glanced around the kitchen, searching for another chore to occupy her mind and steal her time. Unfortunately, there was nothing left but alphabetizing the canned goods, and she refused to be that anal. She'd picked up her grandpa's clutter, scrubbed the sink and cleaned out the fridge. Her territory was, once again, in order.

She wished she could say the same about her life. Days had passed, and she'd garnered a few more signatures by visiting neighbors, but it had become a slow and tedious process. Saturday night at Sparrow's had yielded an additional ten, and she barely had half of what they needed with almost half her time spent. At first glance, it seemed they were right on track, but not if she considered she'd already gathered the easy signatures.

She had to make this work. After her parents had dumped her on her grandpa's doorstep, the grizzled old, scary man had scooped her up and comforted her. She'd been frightened beyond words, and, although she'd needed time before she could fully trust him, he'd saved her.

Now it was her turn to save him.

She opened a pouch of tuna to make a sandwich and pulled pickles and mayonnaise from the fridge. As she mixed the ingredients together, prickly thoughts pestered her. Mostly they were about what Joanna and Laurel had suggested why her grandfather might not want to pursue his dream. His sudden change of attitude made no sense.

Laurel had joked about him having something to hide, but maybe she wasn't far off the mark. Her grandfather had often kidded about his sordid past, but Afton really had no idea what he'd meant other than he'd been a wild teenager. She assumed drinking and probably sex at an early age. Possibly drugs, but that seemed unlikely considering his abhorrence of them now.

He'd grown up in the Kentucky wilderness, hailing from a family of illegal bootleggers. She snorted and shook her head. If Corey knew of her tainted bloodlines, she was certain he and his political aspirations would avoid her like a headline scandal.

She sighed. Johnny Searle. Or was it Johnathan or just John? She really didn't know his actual name. He'd always been Grandpa, and that had been enough.

A knock at the front door startled her. She glanced at the clock as Sonny barked and ran into the living room. Her grandfather had gone to visit a friend and wouldn't be home for a while yet.

She walked to the front of the house and peered through the lace curtain she'd made a few years ago. Mayor Gardiner stood on the porch, studying the house with obvious disdain.

"What on earth?" she whispered. The mayor had never come to her house, and she couldn't imagine why he would now. Thank God, her grandpa wasn't home.

She forced a friendly smile, picked up Sonny so he couldn't get away, and opened the door. "Mayor Gardiner. This is a surprise."

Icy contempt darkened his gaze. "Where is he?"

His tone took her aback, and a fearful shiver slithered over her as Sonny released a low growl. "My grandpa? He's out. Can I help you with something?"

Dwight expelled a sigh, obviously displeased with her answer. Angry intent colored his expression. "I don't know what the hell she could have seen in all this," he muttered.

His words confused her. "Excuse me?"

"You need to talk some sense into that asshole you live with. I'm warning you now. He's messing with fire. I've put up with his shit in the past, but no more." He stabbed a finger in her direction. "Do you hear me? *No more.*"

She took a step back into her house, prepared to slam the door. "I think you should leave."

He pushed forward. "Do you know what you both are to me? Nothing more than a mouse in the grass."

Restrained anger surfaced. She knew she should retreat, but she'd had enough of his bullying. "And you're what? The snake who's going to eat me?"

"I've been compared to worse, Ms. Searle." He narrowed his gaze. "Has a rattler ever bitten you? Ever experienced searing pain as the venom courses through your veins?"

The man had clearly lost his mind. She stepped forward until she was inches from him. She wouldn't cower at this idiot. He might think he was God, but she didn't. "Are you threatening me?"

"Take it however you like."

She'd had enough, and she stared, unblinking. "Mr. Mayor, I'll ask you once again to leave. If you don't step off my porch right now, I'll take it as a personal threat. I have a shotgun, and I know how to use it. That means if you don't want a bullet in your ass, get the hell off my property."

Several tense seconds passed. The hatred burning in his gaze made her wonder if she would have to defend herself.

"I should knock you senseless," he said in a low voice.

She braced herself, and Sonny yipped as though to back her up. *"Try it."*

The mayor pulled back his lips into a sweet, sickening smile that chilled her blood. "It's obvious you came from tainted stock. Tell your grandpa I'm done playing games. He can give me what I want, or I'll tell everyone what I know."

With that, he stalked away.

Afton stared at the dirt road long after the dust from his car had settled. Adrenaline left her shaking as she replayed their insane interaction. The man was unhinged. A vile bastard with one screw loose. That was the only conclusion she could fathom.

Except he seemed certain he had something to hold over her grandpa's head. She wasn't sure she could discount the idea, either. Not with the way Grandpa had been acting.

When she was sure Dwight wouldn't return, Afton shut the door, trying to shake off the emotional slime he'd left behind. She had no idea who he'd meant when he'd mentioned a woman, either.

What she did know was she wouldn't be asking her grandpa or mentioning the mayor's visit at all. That was for damn sure.

Still, she needed answers.

She could no longer pretend something wasn't brewing beneath the surface. Grandpa and the mayor had a history. But how far back did it go and what exactly did the mayor want?

Most of all, what did he know?

Whatever it was, she wouldn't rest until she had the same information.

Her heart thumped as she retrieved her laptop. Maybe she'd find something on the internet. She tried several searches, looking for any reference of them together. When nothing popped up, she continued her search with her grandpa's name only.

Again, she didn't find anything remotely interesting about him or his family from the backwoods of Kentucky. In fact, she hadn't found anything about them, period. She'd known her grandpa's daddy had distrusted the law and preferred to live off the grid, plus records back then, especially in remote areas, hadn't always been recorded or stored properly, so the lack of information wasn't all that surprising.

Maybe the internet was the wrong place to look, knowing the circumstances of his youth. Maybe she'd be better off looking closer to home.

With that, she headed for his bedroom. Guilt nipped at her for snooping, but she needed answers.

An hour later, she emerged, still none the wiser. She couldn't think of another place in the house where he might hide something.

A dark edginess crept into her thoughts until she escaped the confines of the quiet house and stepped into the sunlight, letting Sonny tag along. She needed a break before she drove herself crazy, a moment to reflect on recent events and possible places her grandfather might hide whatever it was Dwight wanted.

Sonny tripped over himself and tumbled down the last two porch steps. "Silly boy," she said as she helped him right himself. He stood on his hind legs and put his soft, fat puppy paws on her hand, giving her a little bark.

The sound of an approaching engine tightened her nerves, and she jerked her gaze upward. She prayed she'd see Grandpa's truck coming down the dirt road and not Dwight's car, but it surprised her to see Laurel's old yellow Jeep instead.

Afton scooped up Sonny to keep him out of the way and waited with a relieved smile on her face until Laurel parked near where she stood. Her fragile happiness evaporated when Laurel emerged from her car, scowling.

"I can't believe you didn't tell me. I'm not kidding this time when I say I wonder if we're still friends." Laurel folded her arms beneath her breasts, her expression warning Afton to come clean or else.

"What are you talking about?" She had a sinking feeling she knew, and she wasn't ready for another emotional altercation so soon.

Laurel shifted her weight to one foot and cocked her hip. "Corey Kendall? A certain heated kiss that took place in broad daylight near Randall's? Really? How could you not tell me?"

Afton slumped against her Jeep with a sigh. "Oh, God."

Laurel approached her. "So, it's true?"

"I don't want it to be. I wish it wasn't. The whole thing freaked me out, and you were talking to Katy when I arrived right after it happened. Then time passed, I calmed down, and I really wanted to forget all about it."

Laurel snorted. "Good luck with that. Old Lady Smith told Jenna Black, who told my mom. No denying it happened, and you know Old Lady Smith will tell everyone."

"Including Mallory O'Brien." Could Afton hope and pray the rumors wouldn't make it to her grandpa? He didn't spend much time in town, but he kept in contact with plenty of people. Anyone could spill.

"Yeah, someone is sure to tell Mallory. That's what Corey gets for messing around. I'm sure she'll dump his ass."

Afton eyed her friend. "He says they're not a couple. That's why he kissed me in public. To prove he was available."

"*What?*" Laurel seemed fascinated with the news. "But I heard they were heavily involved."

Afton attempted a sarcastic look, but she was certain the turmoil hurtling inside her tempered it. "Did you hear that through Old Lady Smith's grapevine, too?"

"Hmm...point taken." Laurel seemed resigned to the fact her argument held no water. "Except the rumor about you *was* apparently true. *What were you thinking*? What happened to your promise to stay clear of anything personal with him? You can't get much more personal than his lips on yours, except..."

"Don't go there, Laurel. I did my best to avoid him. I really did." She could say that with complete honesty. "He's the one who approached me. If I'd have seen him first, I'd have escaped in time. But he caught me off guard. Still, I told him I wouldn't be the other woman in his life, that I respected myself more than that."

"So, he proved there's no one else in his life by kissing you?"

"Yes. But the point is, I tried to push him away, but the more I did, the more he rejected my reasons. I didn't ask for any of this."

Laurel released a wistful sigh. "That's so romantic. Also, he's hot."

Her friend's comments didn't help in the least. "That is *so* not helpful. What the hell should I do now? Our families are at complete odds. He controls my grandpa's future, and my gut says don't trust him."

Right now, she wasn't sure she could trust *anyone*.

Laurel lifted hopeful brows. "Do you have to trust him to date him?"

"Yes. Yes, I do." Afton frowned at her friend. "I can't believe you actually asked that question."

Laurel gave her a guilty shrug. "I know. Shallow. But he's so damn cute. Can't you pretend you trust him? Maybe, eventually, trust will come."

She wished she could adopt Laurel's carefree attitude. "What if I do and he breaks my heart again? Then what? Plus, in the meantime, I would risk pissing off my grandpa enough that he might never speak to me again."

Laurel waved away her excuses. "He'd never do that. You're the center of his universe."

She wasn't so sure. Loyalty was huge in Grandpa's book, and

she'd violated it by rummaging through his things. "There's still the broken heart to consider."

Mischief lit her friend's eyes. "Ha, right? My question is, why do you think you're so special that you shouldn't have to risk your heart like the rest of us? When it comes to love, there are no guarantees."

Laurel's reply stunned her. "I didn't mean it like that. I realize we all take risks. But I'm not in love with him, nor do I want to be. He's the one who kissed me, not the other way around."

"Oh, but he's so cute. If you don't want him, can I have him? I'd risk my heart for a night with him."

Afton rolled her eyes, grateful for the spot of humor. Her friend never let her take anything too seriously. "Yes, you can have him. Take him and keep him out of my sight."

Laurel nudged her arm. "If I could, you know I would. Unfortunately, I'd have to get him to agree, and I'm sure I'm not his type."

"We could kidnap him," Afton offered. "Tie him up and keep him in one of the old caves on my grandpa's land so no one would ever find him."

Her friend pushed back her auburn hair. "Now, you're onto something. What are you doing this afternoon?"

She didn't want to admit to anyone that she'd been searching through her grandfather's things. "Why?"

"Because I'm going to help you with whatever it is that you're doing. My mom is driving me crazy. The longer I stay with you, the happier both of us will be."

"What if your mom shows up here?" Afton said half-teasing, half-serious.

"Highly unlikely."

"No, really. I came home the other night and found her and my grandpa flirting. I'm starting to wonder if there isn't something between them."

Laurel wrinkled her forehead in distaste. "Are you serious?"

Afton couldn't tell if her friend was more surprised or shocked by her statement. "In fact, I'm starting to wonder about a lot of things concerning my grandpa." She exhaled a heavy breath, realizing she needed to have faith that her friend would help her. "I have another confession to make."

Laurel shook her head in mock disappointment. "I'm afraid to ask what now."

All traces of merriment disappeared. "This is serious, Laurel."

Her friend sobered. "Okay. I'm listening."

"The mayor was here a while ago, acting insane."

She scrunched her brows in disbelief. "*What?*"

"He came looking for my grandpa. When I said he wasn't home, he threatened me. So I threatened to get the shotgun."

Her mouth dropped open. "You didn't."

She didn't care who he was. No one threatened her or her grandpa. "I did. I'd do the same again if he comes back."

"*No.* Oh, Afton. You can't shoot the mayor even if he deserves it."

"Trust me. I would have. Before he left, he said to tell my grandpa he'd better give him what he wants, or he'd tell everyone what he knows." Speaking the words aloud was like a punch to her gut.

They both remained silent for a moment, and Afton's worry mirrored in her friend's face. A chill spilled over her. "What do you think he meant?"

"I don't know," Laurel replied. "Could be anything. Could be nothing. If he was talking all kinds of crazy, maybe it's all in his head."

"I would agree, except my grandpa's acting odd, too, and it all started after the council meeting."

"What are you going to do?"

She shrugged. "I don't know, but I must do something. I hate myself for doing it, but I've already searched his room."

"You can't talk to your grandpa about it?"

Afton snorted. "You know I can't." She glanced toward the barn. "He keeps a lot of boxes of crap in the old horse stalls and the tack room. I'm going to look there next, as soon as I find the courage."

Laurel linked her arm with Afton's. "Let's go, then. I'll be your courage."

13

The moment Afton stepped into the barn, a wave of nostalgia washed over her, accompanied by the familiar scents of dust and hay. It was as if the building itself remembered her, holding the memories of her youth within its weathered walls. She'd spent countless hours there, caring for the horse her grandpa had surprised her with one year. She would brush and tend to the majestic creature, muck out the stalls, and lose herself in daydreams about the future that lay ahead.

Those were the days she cherished the most, but they also reminded her of Daisy, the horse she'd lost six years ago. Afton still missed her dearly and held onto the hope that one day she would have a horse again, a companion to share her days with.

With Laurel right behind her, Afton led the way to the small tack room. The room had become a storage space for her grandpa's collection of miscellaneous items, a testament to his reluctance to let go of anything that might prove useful someday.

Wooden crates, weathered by time, lined the interior wall and were stacked neatly like pieces of a puzzle. Each box bore a warning label, hinting at the possibility of explosives hidden within. Afton pulled a crate from the top and set it in the middle of the floor.

Laurel glanced at the box. "Whoa. There's not really dynamite in them, is there?"

Afton chuckled and, as if by instinct, felt along the shelf above the crates until she found the hidden screwdriver. "No, there's no dynamite," she reassured her friend. "My grandpa used these boxes to transport his belongings out west when he was younger. They belonged to his grandfather, and he found them cool, so he decided to keep them. As far as I know, he uses them to store old tools and papers. I've never really delved deeper into it. There was never a need to."

Laurel nodded solemnly, understanding the weight of the situation. "But now, you do."

Afton crouched near one of the old wooden boxes, her fingers gripping the screwdriver tightly. "I need to uncover what's going on."

"And you think the answers might be in here?" She put a hand on her hip, jutting it out like she always did, sounding exactly like an inquisitive journalist.

Afton bit her lip as she pondered Laurel's question. "I hope so," she finally responded with a sigh. "Before I push ahead, I want to make sure the mayor is the senseless one, and there are no family demons ready to burst into daylight if I open the wrong proverbial box."

Afton grunted and shoved the screwdriver in farther. The lid came free with a rush, and she fell back on her butt on the cement floor.

Peering over Afton's shoulder, Laurel examined the contents of the box, unsure of what to make of them. "I don't think there are any family ghosts in there."

Afton, now on her knees, gazed into the box filled with metal parts, including copper tubing turned green with age and a rusted spigot. "Looks like parts of an ancient still, maybe."

That piqued Laurel's curiosity, and she reached into the box and pulled out the spigot, turning it over in her palm. "As in a moonshine still?"

"You know as well as I do that it's been the family business for generations," Afton said with a laugh.

"Yeah, but your grandpa only makes a few bottles for the locals." She glanced up, her eyes bright with interest. "*This* could have been used to make cases of illegal moonshine back in the day, maybe by your great-grandpa, when they would make midnight trips and outrun the law. Do you know anything about him? Have you ever checked out your family history?"

Regret tumbled through Afton, and she shook her head.

Laurel's gaze wandered off, lost in thought, as she seemed to contemplate the possibilities that lay within Afton's family history. "There's so much hidden within these old walls," she murmured. "Stories untold, secrets waiting to be discovered. You once said your grandpa had moved here from Kentucky. Weren't there lots of hillbillies brewing *white lightning* in the hills? Or was that in Tennessee? I should have paid better attention in history class."

Afton frowned and took the spigot from Laurel, placing it back in the box before she used the butt of the screwdriver to pound the lid in place.

"*What?*" Laurel asked, looking bewildered.

"What if my family *is* a bunch of renegade hillbillies? Then what?" The thought left her anxious.

Laurel shook her head, trying to soothe her worries. "Who cares? Prohibition happened back in the twenties, a century ago. This stuff looks old, too. Your grandpa is a decent man. With a bit of a shady side. But he's not brewing tons of whiskey in the back-woods and trying to outrun the law. Do you think he would have considered getting a permit if he didn't have a clear record? I don't think so."

Laurel made a ton of sense, and it eased her fears somewhat. "Probably not. I think between my grandpa acting so weird and this whole thing with Corey, I may have temporarily misplaced my sanity. Just like the mayor."

"Happens to the best of us." Laurel eyed the stack of crates. "Are you sure you don't want to look inside more of them? We might not find the answers you're seeking, but this old stuff is really cool."

Afton hesitated, but her curious side won. "Okay, maybe one more. It is my family history, after all." She pulled down another and pried off the lid.

"Oh," Laurel said with a frown as she peered at the contents. Layers of paper, yellowed and faded by time, filled the box. She lifted the top sheets and examined them. "There's not much left here to see. I hope they weren't important."

"I hope not either." Afton gently removed another stack, carefully shuffling through them. "This one is still legible. It's a bill of sale for a 1969 Ford truck. To John Allan...Searcy."

Laurel leaned closer. "Searcy? Not Searle?"

Afton stared at the name in front of her. "Searcy." She glanced at Laurel with raised brows, wanting her to erase the troubled feeling brewing in her mind.

"That's interesting." Laurel moved to her side and viewed the legal document. Then she pulled another from beneath that one, but the writing was once again faded. "Nothing here."

"What do you think it means?" What she really wanted to know was why would her grandfather change his name, but she couldn't voice those words.

"Doesn't necessarily mean anything. Could be a typo. Anything else in there?"

Afton shuffled through the rest of the stack, coming upon a pay stub for John A. Searle.

"See? Just a typo. Stop freaking yourself out." Laurel placed a hand on her hip again. "Have you bothered to ask your grandpa what might be wrong? You should before jumping to conclusions. I think you should tell him about the mayor's visit, too."

Her question caused Afton to pause. "I can't do that. He'll go ballistic and truly will shoot the mayor."

"Then ask about the other stuff."

Obviously, Laurel didn't know how stubborn her grandfather was. "He won't open up to me. Of that, I'm sure."

"I think you shouldn't discount it until you try. You never know. If he truly needs help, he might. Promise me you'll ask him."

A rumbling truck engine sounded outside, and Afton pursed her lips. "He's home."

Laurel sent her a sly smile. "Good. There's no time like the present."

She hesitated to respond, and then sighed. She wasn't sure she was up for the fight. "Fine. I'll ask." But, as sure as the sun would rise in the morning, her grandfather would never confide in or lean on her.

"I'll pick you up at about five to head to Sparrow's, okay?" Laurel said as she headed for her jeep.

Of course, after exacting a promise from Afton that she'd talk to her grandpa, Laurel wouldn't stick around and give her a reason to postpone the conversation. "Uh-huh. See you then."

Unease slithered through Afton as Laurel said hi and goodbye to her grandpa as he exited his truck. On the surface, it seemed a simple conversation with her grandfather should clear up everything. But her instincts warned that by attempting it, she'd be walking into a rattler's den.

———

Early afternoon sun enhanced Corey's mood as it poured through the open window of his midnight blue, late-edition Dodge truck. Twice now, he'd found opportunities to kiss Afton again. As amazing as that had been, he'd learned it wasn't nearly enough. He wanted more.

He glanced at the rolled set of plans and tried to distract himself by mentally reviewing the checklist of what he needed to present to the planning commission in Pinecone. They'd personally asked him to submit drawings for the new combined administration building and library they intended to build the following year.

That they'd sought him out spoke volumes about how far he'd come developing his design business. He'd worked damn hard the past couple of years to gain a reputation of creating beautiful, yet functional designs.

As he passed City Hall, headed for the open road between Aspen and Pinecone, his phone rang. Dwight Gardiner's name popped up on the screen in his truck, and he tapped the answer button. "What can I do for you, Mayor?"

"Do you have a moment you could stop by my office?" Dwight asked.

"I'm headed out of town for an important meeting. Can it wait?"

"I know. I just saw you drive past. Turn your truck around and stop for a minute. I'll meet you at the front steps of City Hall."

Corey glanced at the clock and mentally groaned. Unfortunately, he had plenty of time. "Be right there."

He made a U-turn and pulled in front of Aspen's main building where Dwight stood, trying to look dignified in a suit that was at least one size too small for his potbelly. Corey climbed out, his dress boots smacking the asphalt as they touched down.

"Thanks for taking a few minutes," Dwight said, extending his hand.

"No problem. Is this something Larry should be here for, too?" More than that, did whatever they were about to discuss need to be conducted in an open meeting?

"Nah, just some personal business." Dwight smiled, but instead of inspiring cordial feelings, his gesture left Corey on edge. Dwight nodded toward a park bench off to the side of the entrance, and they headed in that direction.

"I don't have much time," Corey said as Dwight folded his large frame onto the iron bench.

"This won't take long. Heard a rumor today that disturbed me a might bit."

Corey continued to stand. "Something to do with the new housing project? Wait. Never mind. You said it was personal."

"I've had several people stop by my office concerned about our newest council member."

He snorted. "Me? Why?"

"Hilda Lawler spotted you *making out on the street corner like a teenager,* I believe she said." He lifted questioning brows full of fire. "With none other than Afton Searle. Imagine that. Especially after you said you weren't sleeping with her and all. Hilda didn't think that was appropriate behavior for someone now representing the interests of our town."

He had to be joking. "You realize Hilda is Kirk Lawler's mother, don't you? And that the Pinecone Planning Commission chose my firm over his for their new admin building?" The pettiness of some people really pissed him off.

Dwight darkened his gaze. "Are you disagreeing with the facts as she presented them?"

His irritation inched toward anger. "What I do with my personal time is my *personal* business."

"Until you step into the political arena. Then it becomes

everyone's business." Dwight stood and put his hand on Corey's shoulder in a father-like gesture. "Look son, I mean this in the friendliest way. You have a bright future ahead of you, thanks to your daddy. *Don't* screw it up by messing with the wrong woman. John Searle is as dirty as they come, and you don't want his mud on you. It could cost you not only your place on the council, but it could affect your business as well."

Corey glanced around, wishing someone had heard the mayor's offensive words. "That sounds like a threat, Dwight. Are you saying if I don't play your way, bad things will happen?"

The mayor shrugged. "I've been around long enough to know the way the cookie crumbles. Play the game or lose. That's how it is. Really, it's only a matter of time before some authority gets wind of Searle's activities and is willing to come looking. Just because our sheriff's department needs to pull their heads out of their asses, doesn't mean ATF or the Department of Alcoholic Beverage Control won't investigate. Honestly, I'm surprised someone hasn't notified them by now."

Another threat? "ABC already approved their license."

"They wouldn't have if they'd known what they're up to."

He gasped at the man's audacity. "Can you prove it, Dwight? Do you think someone like ATF is going to waste their resources on a small-time operation like his if the local sheriff can't be bothered?"

All traces of friendliness between them evaporated. "I'm saying if Johnny Searle keeps pushing this petition of his, it will backfire in his face. And it's going to hurt a lot worse than he's expecting. Stay out of it, son. Stay out of her pants. Don't let something that's only worth a quick roll in the hay ruin your life. Understand?"

Corey exhaled a deep breath as he fought to maintain his composure. He wanted to explode like a fireball into a vat of gunpowder, but he would take the high ground. "I understand your threats and your unfair judgments. Now, I need you to understand this. I consider you a friend, Dwight. Hell, you were one of the men I've always looked up to, but I *don't* bow to threats, and I can't be bought. I make my own decisions, and I'll *damn well* spend time with any person I want. With that parting sentiment, I'll see you around."

He stood and strode toward his truck, anger fueling his steps.

"You're making a mistake," Dwight called after him.

He extended his middle finger into the air as he kept walking. The moment he did, he regretted it. He'd let his emotions goad him into an immature gesture that would be splashed all over the papers if anyone had captured the picture.

"Shit," he hissed as he jerked open his truck door. He glanced at Dwight as he started the engine. The mayor stood on the steps of City Hall, staring directly at him as he spoke into his phone.

The way Dwight stood straight, his piercing gaze pinned on Corey, left him with an uneasy feeling. He'd come across many bullies in his life, but he'd certainly never expected to encounter it in this form.

Half a mile down the road, his phone rang again. He didn't recognize the number, but answered it anyway. As the chairman of the Pinecone Planning Commission spoke, Corey lifted his foot off the gas, slowing down his truck and eventually coming to a stop along the side of the road.

"No, I understand. Is this decision final?" Corey asked in response as cold awareness gripped him. "Okay, then. Thank you."

He sat in his truck for several long minutes, barely noticing the green rolling alfalfa fields surrounding him. His pulse thundered in his head, and it took time before he calmed. The only way he could control his emotions was to block the heated, vengeful thoughts from his mind.

He punched in a number on his truck's console and waited for the phone to connect.

"Jerry," he said when his friend answered. "How about you and Kim meet me at Sparrow's about five-thirty or six? I need a strong drink of whiskey in order to make sense of today."

"Damn, Corey. That doesn't sound good. Let me check with the wife. If you don't hear from me, I'll be there."

"Thanks, buddy. I appreciate it."

From experience, he knew if he didn't get his thoughts clear, then he was bound to do something he'd regret. Jerry, with his tactical mind, could view the circumstances without emotion and help him work out reasonable next moves.

Because he didn't intend to take Dwight's attack lying down.

14

As the once fearsome and strong Johnny Searle crossed the gravel, walking from his truck toward the house, Afton forced herself to smile, intent on doing her best to get him to open up. "Have a good day?" she asked.

"It was all right," he grumbled.

She stepped in beside him as he headed toward the front porch. He seemed awfully weary from spending the morning with one of his buddies. "Where did you guys go?"

"Places."

"*Places?*" Sarcasm had slipped into her answer before she could stop it.

His boots stopped crunching the gravel as he halted and eyed her with a look that would have sent her running for her room as a child.

"Sorry." She gave him a placating smile. "What I meant was, I'm curious about what you guys did. Didn't mean to pry."

He gave her a brief nod of forgiveness, his face pale and taut. "Sometimes a man isn't in the mood to talk, dumplin'."

His reply, or lack of, worried her even more. "Are you okay? You look pale."

"I'm fine, but I could use some peace." Which meant stop asking questions.

She swallowed the thick lump at the back of her throat and walked silently next to him as they approached the house. He held open the door for her and Sonny, and she stepped inside.

"We now have fifty-one people who've signed the petition," she said, trying again for a civilized conversation.

A hint of a smile fleetingly crossed his lips as he removed his denim jacket and hung it over the back of a chair near the front door. "Yeah?" he asked, his color returning.

Her mood brightened with his interest. "Yep. Every person I've asked has been more than happy to sign."

He nodded, his satisfaction evident. "Have you asked Wayne Staker? I know he'll back me."

"Not yet. I'm planning to drive out to the company office on Monday and ask all the guys then." She made a mental note to add that to her list of potential advocates. "Luke Winchester and his dad both signed, though."

He wrinkled his brows in surprise. "I'll be damned."

"We can win this, Grandpa. So many people want to support you, and I think that shows what kind of man you are."

He shot her a skeptical look. "If that ass Gardiner wasn't standing in my way, I'd feel better about the whole deal."

"You're not afraid of him." Not her grandpa.

But the moment she said it, a thread of fear whipped across his expression, and then disappeared a second later, increasing her worry tenfold. Dammit.

She hated the uncertainty churning inside her. "Dwight can't do anything. Not with the support of the people. If we get enough signatures, they'll have to let us proceed. Otherwise, we could sue for it. We have the state on board, and we'll get a majority in town, too. This is going to happen."

He sighed, looking old and weary, which scared her. "It's a

great plan, Afton. Makes me happy to dream about it. But remember what I said about keeping it reasonable. I don't want to rile Gardiner too much."

He lowered into his favorite recliner, not caring that the once-forest green fabric had worn to a dull shade of gray. "I didn't expect to encounter his resistance, but maybe I should have. I really don't want to put my energy into fighting a battle against him right now."

She approached him and sat on the arm of the chair, hoping he'd talk with her or at least give her a clue. "What are you talking about? What's up with Gardiner?"

"Nothing but shit. He don't like it because I don't like him, and I'm not afraid to tell people that."

She waited for him to explain further, but he didn't. "You don't have to worry about putting all your energy into this, you know. If there are things you don't want to handle, just tell me. I can do them, or find someone who will. We'll have to hire people eventually, and I know Laurel will help us out with the petition."

His laugh came out in a deep, sad rumble. "An old man and two girls. Just how far do you think we'll get?"

Afton frowned, showing him her displeasure. "I'm not a girl. I'm a woman. A college-educated woman who also has a dream of owning a whiskey distillery, who's not about to be pushed around by some fat, old bureaucrat." She paused for a breath. "Dammit."

He made a mocking bow from his seat. "I beg your pardon, miss."

She needed to press the issue, and there was no time like the present. She gave him a sad smile. "I'm serious, Grandpa. This means as much to me as it does...or did to you. I don't understand why you don't seem to care anymore, and why you say you should have expected Dwight to fight you. I didn't realize you'd even ever had a conversation with the man."

He blinked a few times and then stood. "We had a misunderstanding years ago. The slimy bastard tried to pull one over on me and didn't like it when I caught him. Didn't like it when I told others, either."

"Then tell me why you've lost your fight all the sudden. My grandpa would never back down to an overbearing jerk like Dwight Gardiner." She hoped her use of colorful language would light a fire inside him. She couldn't bear to think he was fading. "He would fight."

Frustration warred with irritation on his face until the anger remained. "I'm not backing down because of that asshole."

"Then why?" she pushed.

He stared at her for a moment, his gaze darkening until it matched the black strands still left in his hair. "Because I don't want it anymore, okay? Not like I used to."

Her world continued to shift like an active fault line. "I don't believe you."

He straightened. "You calling me a liar?"

Once again, his admonishing look left her feeling like a child. "Of course not. I just want you to talk to me. Tell me what's wrong."

"There's nothing wrong other than you calling me a liar." The anger she'd hoped he'd show against Gardiner stood strong in his face.

"I'm not calling you a liar. I just want us to talk."

"As far as I can tell, girl, we've been talking. Up until you insulted me. Now, we're finished." He struggled out of his creaking recliner and stomped from the room toward the kitchen. She knew better than to follow.

A few moments later, the back door slammed, followed by the sound of his truck engine firing up. She hurried to the window. Instead of heading toward the main road, he drove around the side of the house and up into the hills.

She growled her frustration, making Sonny whimper. She

shifted her attention to the puppy, who sat at her feet. His brown eyes filled with worry as his little tail thumped against the floor in agitation.

She scooped him up and kissed his soft head. "I'm sorry, buddy. We didn't mean to scare you. But it makes me so mad when he does that. He didn't want to answer my questions, so he caused a fight just so he could leave. It's an underhanded tactic, and it pisses me off."

Sonny lifted his ears as though he'd understood.

"You're so cute." She stared into his sweet face, making him wiggle with excitement. "And you know what it's like to be left alone, don't you?"

She'd always hated it when her grandpa avoided a confrontation and left instead. Especially when he was angry. He'd disappear into the wooded area for hours, leaving her alone in the house to cry or fret.

When he returned, he usually seemed happier, but the time in between had been hell. Especially right after she'd come to live with him. The first time he'd left after her parents had dropped her on his doorstep, she thought he'd walked out on her, too.

She'd never told him how painful those excruciating hours had been, nor how overwhelmingly relieved she'd been that he'd returned. In the years since, she'd grown curious about where he went. He'd often come back smelling of whiskey, so she'd figured he must have a stash somewhere.

Perhaps he kept whatever the mayor wanted there. Perhaps that would be the next place she investigated.

She sighed and let the curtain drop. He'd come home later when he'd soothed his restless soul. Right now, she needed something to ease her own worries. She'd done what Laurel had suggested, and it had gotten her nowhere. Just as she'd suspected.

Antagonized by his stubborn refusal to talk to her, she rationalized her next moves. She wasn't one to sit and worry and not do what she could. He was the one who refused to talk and left her with no choice but to use other means to find information. Privacy be damned.

She entered her bedroom and grabbed her laptop before climbing onto her bed. Her previous internet search hadn't given her much. But now she had more information to work with.

Her fingers clicked the keys until "John Searcy Kentucky" appeared in the browser on her screen. The first entry she discovered was an article from a small-town newspaper in Franklin County, Kentucky.

Johnny Searcy, seventeen years old, had been convicted for petty theft. The article went on to explain how this person, who may or may not be her grandfather, had stolen gas from a local merchant. He'd also been caught with illegal alcohol substances in his vehicle, but the prosecutor had apparently dismissed those charges when Mr. Searcy pled guilty to the other.

Could that person have been her grandfather? If so, was this why he'd changed his name? She wasn't thrilled that he'd stolen from others, but he'd mentioned his rough upbringing a few times. She could understand how someone who'd still been a kid might get involved in things he shouldn't. It wasn't the end of the world.

Certainly not enough to cause a person to change his name.

She scrolled down farther and clicked on another archived article from the same newspaper. Her laptop responded with a startling discovery that ripped through her mind and left her heart racing. *One man left dead while county police hunt for John Searcy, believing he could provide answers.*

She placed a hand over her stomach, wanting to calm the churning inside. That man couldn't possibly be her grandpa. Her grandfather might be rough on the outside, but he was smart and kind. Not a killer.

She couldn't begin to believe that about him. Wouldn't believe it. Ever.

Her grandpa's odd behavior had set her on edge. That was all. Didn't make him a murderer. They didn't even have the same last name.

She glanced at the clock and closed her computer. She needed to stop worrying and get ready for an evening of gathering more signatures. She barely had two weeks left to complete her petition or all their hard work had been for nothing.

Otherwise, their jerk of a mayor would win, and she couldn't let that happen.

15

Laurel pulled her yellow Jeep into the parking lot at Sparrow's, and Afton tugged her pretty pink skirt into place before climbing out. The evening was warmer than she'd expected, and she unzipped her black leather jacket to make herself more comfortable.

"I'm glad we dressed up," Laurel said with a laugh. She'd worn a short black dress and cowboy boots that crunched the gravel as they headed toward the sidewalk in front of Sparrow's.

Afton handed a clipboard to her friend. "I thought it would be a good idea to look like I could run a business. If we push the appeal through, the people who sign could also be my future customers. By the way, I called Becky earlier to make sure Sparrow's didn't have a problem with us setting up camp outside."

"Okay, good." Laurel tossed her auburn hair over her shoulder. "How did the talk go with your grandpa?"

Afton grimaced. "What talk? He stomped out the second I pressed for answers."

Worry creased her friend's forehead. "I'm sorry, but don't give up. We'll figure this out. Besides, I have a good feeling about tonight."

Afton latched onto her friend's enthusiasm. "That's because you look hot in your little black dress, and you know it."

"Whatever," Laurel said with a laugh.

"I couldn't agree more," said a masculine voice from behind them. She and Laurel turned to see Jerry and the same guy Afton had seen him with before approaching from the parking lot.

The stranger's eyes sparked with interest as he assessed Laurel, while his raven black hair gave him a mysterious air. "What's your name, darlin'?"

An overly friendly smile appeared on Laurel's face that Afton recognized as trouble. "If you want to know, that's going to cost you...*darlin'*."

He sauntered closer, looking down at her, his expression letting her know he was up for the challenge. "I'll give you anything you want. Name it."

Afton shared a glance with Jerry, and they both tried to hide their smiles. The guy couldn't know what he was getting into.

She shoved a clipboard into his hands. "First, I'd like you to sign your name on this line here."

He studied the paper. "What is it?"

"What difference does it make?" Laurel tossed back at him. "You said you'd give me anything I want. Sign it."

"It's a petition to help my grandpa get a permit to open a whiskey distillery in Aspen," Afton supplied, not wanting any disputes about the validity of the signatures they collected.

"Sure," he said, giving her a nod.

Laurel cleared her throat to regain his attention before thrusting a pen at him.

He took his time slipping the pen from her grasp, lacing the exchange with sexual overtones. Afton had to hand it to her friend, though. She didn't blink or blush once.

When he finished, he handed the clipboard to her, and Laurel glanced at it. "Charlie. Thank you for your support."

Afton slipped her hand in to claim the clipboard and passed it to Jerry.

Charlie tilted his head. "You're welcome, darlin'. Now, how about your name? I'll even take your number."

Jerry groaned as he finished signing his name, drawing a glance from Charlie before he looked at Laurel.

Laurel gave him her brightest smile. "Will you now?"

Charlie narrowed his gaze, seeming to catch on that things were not quite what he'd hoped. He glanced at all of them. "What?"

Jerry clapped him on the back. "Come on, buddy, before you lose one of your balls."

As Jerry walked toward the door, Charlie snatched Laurel's hand and kissed it. "Fine, darlin'. Play hard to get. But I guarantee before the end of the night, you'll give me your name."

She laughed, her happiness genuine, and Afton realized the guy might have a chance after all. "Don't count on it."

He backed toward the door. "Oh, I'm counting. I still have almost seven hours before tomorrow. That's more than enough time to win you over."

Afton watched her friend stare at the door until both men had disappeared inside. "Wow. He was quite the flirt. Cute, too."

"Too much flirt. Too much cute." Laurel's complaints came with a smile.

"You like him." That fact was more than obvious.

"Doesn't matter. A guy like him leaves a flood of broken hearts in his wake." Laurel turned and looked down the street as though she actually might see his conquests.

Afton wondered if he was a younger version of Sam, a man who couldn't pick one woman and keep her. A soft breeze kicked up, and she closed her jacket around her. "Some woman, someday, will tame him."

Laurel laughed. "Maybe. But who knows how long that will

be and how many hearts he'll break before then? He'd be a fun challenge, but I prefer a solid, steady man I can trust."

"They seem in short supply in Aspen," Afton said as she turned her back to the street the second that she spotted Corey's truck. "Here comes another questionable one right now."

"Come on. You know you like the guy. Give him a chance," Laurel said. "Plus, he's adorable, and he likes you."

Afton wanted to smack her friend as she watched Corey drive his truck into the parking lot. "Stop staring at him."

"Can't. He's too beautiful."

She glanced down the street and then at the front door to Sparrow's, trapped with nowhere to run without being obvious. "Oh, God. I need to go hide."

Laurel linked her arm through Afton's, preventing her from leaving. "He already saw you. If you leave, he'll know you're avoiding him."

She tried to tug her arm free, deciding avoidance and humiliation were better than facing him, but Laurel grasped her tighter. "Do I care? No. Let him think what he wants."

"Your hearts have collided, and you're going to have to figure this out. Can't hide from it. Hello, Councilmember Kendall," she called out the moment he stepped from his truck. "Nice to see you this evening."

"Hi, Laurel," he said as he approached. "Please call me, Corey."

"Of course." Her laugh was a tad too flirtatious for Afton's comfort.

"Evening, Afton." He glanced at the clipboard. "Looks like you're hard at work again."

"As a matter of fact." Awkwardness stole her cool, and she thrust the petition toward him without considering his position in town. "How about you? Would you care to sign to support my grandfather's business?"

He gave her a dangerously sexy smile. "I don't think that's a wise idea."

"Really? Who better than one of the lawmakers?"

His gaze softened. "It might negate your petition, Afton. Those opposing your grandfather's permit might say my signature generated undue support in your favor. Casting a shadow of doubt on your efforts will ultimately hurt you."

"He's right, Afton," Laurel interjected in a pleasant voice, and Afton knew she was trying to diffuse the situation. "All we ask is for fair consideration from the council once we have the petition."

He shifted his gaze to Afton. "That I can promise you," he said softly, sincerity in his eyes.

She wanted to continue to be agitated with him, but couldn't. "Thank you for that, then. Don't let us keep you from your evening."

Corey raised hopeful brows. "I'd love it if you'd join me and my friends when you finish here."

"Not likely," Afton said before Laurel could agree. "I'm sure we'll head home once we finish."

He stared at her for a long moment, trying to communicate through a look, but she blinked and glanced away. "Okay, then. I wish you luck with your endeavors. I'm sure few will resist your lovely charms."

"Thanks," Laurel said with a rush of enthusiasm.

Afton sent him a small smile and then watched as he turned and entered Sparrow's. The moment he was out of sight, she exhaled. As long as he stayed out of her way, she'd handle the rest of her night very well.

Two hours later, she and Laurel had nearly filled another two sheets. Unfortunately, the number of potential advocates had started to dwindle since most people who'd come to watch the live band had already arrived.

"Sixteen more people," Afton said, the thrill of victory warming her veins.

Laurel bounced up and down on her heels, rubbing her hands over her arms. "That's awesome. We're going to do this, you know?"

Afton couldn't stop her grin. "I think so, too. I can't wait to tell Grandpa when we pull it off. You know, he called us *girls*, saying he and a couple of girls couldn't win this battle."

Laurel snorted. "I guess we'll show him then, won't we? Hey, I'm going inside for a minute. I really need to use the ladies' room and warm my bones. If you're okay, I'll be back in a few."

Afton glanced up and down the mostly empty street. "Pretty sure I can handle it on my own."

After Laurel left, Afton snuggled deeper into her leather jacket. Spring days in Aspen quickly lost their heat after the sun disappeared. A lone pair of headlights curved around the nearby bend and headed her way. As the vehicle approached, she waved, trying to be friendly to everyone.

The flash of blue and red lights startled her, and she realized she'd waved to a deputy in an unmarked vehicle. As he circled around and pulled next to the curb, she groaned.

A man she recognized as the mayor's nephew stepped out of the dark blue sedan and headed toward her.

Something about the look in his eye set her on edge, and she prayed he was more reasonable than his uncle. "Evening, officer. Is there a problem?"

The buff-looking cop with an attitude to match stared her down. "May I see your identification, ma'am?"

She narrowed her gaze, damn sure he recognized her. "It's me, Karl. Afton Searle."

He stared at her with hard eyes. "I'll need to see your I.D."

"Okay..." She scrambled, trying to figure out his angle. "My purse is in Laurel's Jeep, and she's inside the bar. I'll just go get her."

When she turned to walk away, he grabbed her arm to stop her. Instinct kicked in, and she swung at him in a defensive gesture. Before her heart could resume beating, he had her pinned against the sedan, her arms behind her.

His voice was breathless, excited. "Assaulting an officer is a serious offense, ma'am."

The cold metal of his vehicle burned through her skirt as panic tumbled her thoughts. "I didn't try to assault you, Karl. You grabbed me. It was a reflex."

He cuffed her and stepped back.

She turned in a whirl of fury. "Take these off me right now. I haven't done anything wrong."

"Loitering. Soliciting. Assaulting an officer."

Frustration rose inside her, and she struggled against the cuffs. "What the hell are you talking about?"

He held her with a piercing gaze as he pressed the mic attached to his shoulder and said some mumbo jumbo police talk that she didn't understand.

The dispatcher responded. "Copy that." He leveled a stern look at her, and she wished she could rip out his eyes.

Her pulse increased as he opened the rear passenger door. "Dammit, Karl. You'd better let me go, or you know this will come back to bite you in the ass."

He gripped her by the arm. "We can do this the easy way or the hard way, but either way, I'm taking you in."

She jerked free and strode toward the bar, though she wasn't sure how she'd open the door. "The hell you are."

He caught her and hauled her around, nearly pulling her arm from her socket.

She screamed as he dragged her toward the car.

He grunted as she continued to fight him. "Don't make me add resisting arrest to the charges."

"*Help me*," she screamed again, though there was no one to hear her.

He shoved her inside and slammed the door. A few seconds later, he climbed into the driver's seat and pulled away.

Tears came as she fought to make sense of the last few minutes. "This is because of your uncle, isn't it? You know this is wrong, Karl. I can't tell you how many ways this will come back to haunt you."

The deputy remained silent, refusing to engage as he shifted the car into gear. She bit into her bottom lip, wishing the pain would chase away her tears. She'd have to wait until she reached the jail in Pinecone before she could call Laurel to let her know what had happened. Unfortunately, her friend would freak out when she returned outside to find she'd disappeared without a trace.

If Afton didn't know it before, she did now. Dwight Gardiner played dirty, and she couldn't help but wonder if her grandpa had backed down to protect her.

16

Corey spotted Laurel the second she walked in the door. Mostly because he'd been watching who came in all night, hoping Afton would change her mind. Unfortunately, she didn't come in behind Laurel.

"Hey." Jerry nudged Charlie. "Look who's here."

Charlie cranked his head and grinned. "Yeah, baby. I knew she couldn't stay away."

He and Jerry both barked a laugh.

"Are you kidding, Charlie?" Corey shook his head. "Laurel—"

"Don't say her name," Charlie said, cutting him off. "I want her to tell me."

Jerry shook his head. "I already tried to tell him about her, Corey. He won't listen."

"That's right," Charlie said and stood. "Watch how it's done, gentlemen. Watch how it's done."

Charlie sauntered over and caught Laurel near the end of the bar. It was too loud to hear their conversation, but a moment later, Charlie stepped aside and let Laurel head down the hall.

Corey raised his brows at Charlie in a taunting question, and Charlie quickly gave him the thumbs up.

"Looks like he's going to have to wait for her to pee," Jerry said with a laugh.

Corey joined in. "I think she'll make him wait for a hell of a lot more than that."

"You're one to talk. The two of you have been surveilling the front door all night, waiting for Afton or Laurel to come inside." Jerry gave him a look that dared him to deny it.

Corey shrugged. He didn't care who knew.

"You sure you know what you're doing?" Jerry asked.

He knew what he wanted, but the path between him and Afton was rocky at best. He laughed. "No."

Jerry lifted a casual shoulder. "Seems to me if you have something to hide, maybe you shouldn't be messing with her. Didn't we learn that well enough in our younger years?"

"I'm not the one hiding. She is. She's afraid of her grandfather's reaction."

"To you?" He snorted. "You're harmless."

"Johnny Searle detests authority in any shape or form. Plus, the council denied his permit to operate inside the city limits, which he's currently disputing."

Jerry lifted his brows in disbelief. "And you want to date his granddaughter? Dude, you really are asking for trouble."

Maybe he did need to have his head examined. "That's not the worst of it. Gardiner's not happy about it either. We had a pissing match earlier today. That's what I wanted to talk to you about. He threatened my livelihood if I continued to see her."

Jerry narrowed his eyes into an incredulous look. "*What*?"

"He didn't just threaten. He followed through. After talking to him, I told him what I thought of his suggestion and left. I saw him on the phone as I pulled away, and a minute later, I got a call from Pinecone's Planning Commission letting me know they no longer required my services."

Jerry shook his head. "That's bullshit. Didn't you sign an

agreement with them? A contract for services before you started working on the project?"

"It was in progress. I wasn't worried about payment because they're a government agency."

He cussed beneath his breath. "And now you're screwed. All because of a girl."

His pulse raced with ire. "It's not Afton's fault. It's because of Gardiner. I'll stand up to him any day of the week if I don't agree with him. I won't be a pawn in his manipulative game, and I can't be bought. It has nothing to do with Afton. She just happens to be the catalyst."

"Okay," Jerry said with a laugh. "Tell me how you really feel."

"Screw you," he volleyed with a sarcastic whisper, chiding his friend for teasing him about a serious matter. "Besides, Afton isn't just any girl."

"I can see that."

"Yeah? The way I could see that about you when you swore that you'd never speak to Kimber again after she deserted you?"

A smile crossed his lips, and he dipped his head. "Touché."

"What I need is to figure out my next move. I've gotta be smart, though. Gardiner's been at this a lot longer than I have."

Jerry snorted. "Whatever you do, just know I have your back. I have a feeling you're going to need it."

The cloud of anxiety that had been trailing him all day grew darker. "I hate to say it, but you might be right."

The front door opened again, and two men rushed in, looking frantically around. By the looks on their faces, something was wrong.

"Where's Laurel?" One of them yelled. "Anyone seen Laurel? Deputy Karl just threw Afton into his police car and sped off. We were in the parking lot when we heard her screaming."

"*What the hell?*" Corey was on his feet before he could think. He rushed over to the two men. "What happened?"

He listened to their story, his anger growing with each word. They didn't know much, other than Gardiner's nephew had kidnapped Afton from the side of the street for no obvious reason.

Laurel joined them, her face heavy with worry. "What's going on? I heard someone yelling for me."

"Thanks," he told the two men and pulled Laurel away. "Come with me." He motioned for Jerry and Charlie to follow as he headed out the front door.

He scrubbed the whiskers on his jaw as the four of them assembled outside, and he filled them in on the details. "I know what this is about. The slimy mayor is playing dirty, and it needs to end."

"What are you talking about?" Laurel asked. *"The mayor did this?"*

Corey mentally unloaded a string of curses. "Bet your sweet ass that he's the one behind it. What other reason would a deputy have to arrest Afton?"

Laurel shook her head. "None. But he can't do that, can he?"

"You'd be surprised what someone in power can do if he chooses," Jerry answered.

Laurel blew out a breath. "I don't know if Afton would want me to tell you, but the mayor came to her house today and threatened her, too."

Corey feared he might explode. *"What?"*

Laurel nodded, her expression full of fear. "He warned her to watch out for a snake that would bite her if she didn't get her grandpa to give him what he wanted. Though, neither of us knows what the mayor wants, and her grandpa isn't talking."

Corey had heard all he needed to. "This is such bullshit. I'm going to Pinecone to see what I can do. I know an excellent lawyer in town. He'll have her out tonight. The mayor isn't the only one who has influence. Laurel, call her grandfather. Tell him not to worry, that she's staying with you tonight. We don't need him barreling down there and getting himself locked up, too."

The panic in her face increased. "He'll want to know why she's not calling herself."

"Make up something," he said, itching to be on his way. "Say she drank too much and passed out. Anything is better than the truth at this point."

"You're right." She nodded. "If he finds out what happened, he'll come unglued. That won't be good for any of us."

Charlie waved him onward. "Don't worry about things here. We've got it covered."

"Thanks." Corey gave them a nod and strode toward the parking lot. "I'll call when I know something."

———

Afton sat in the lonely, cold cell, surrounded by cement and fears about her future. For nearly three hours, she'd relived the events of the evening. She deeply regretted waving at Karl and wondered if it would have made a difference if she hadn't.

Solicitation? Seriously? There was no way that would hold up in court. The other two charges...maybe. She wished she understood the law better, but she had to believe she was within her right to stand on a public street and ask for signatures. She hadn't done anything wrong.

Except punch Karl, but he'd deserved that.

She needed a lawyer. But before she could secure one, she needed them to let her make a damn phone call so she could get the hell out of there.

She stood and glanced into the empty corridor outside her cell. "Hello?" she yelled.

"Shut up," responded a male voice. "No one cares."

She exhaled a heavy breath and paced the length of her small cell. Noises down the hall stopped her, and she struggled to peer through the iron bars to see who made them.

A moment later, a female deputy with short brown hair stopped in front of her cell and slid a key into the lock.

"Do I get to make my phone call now?" Afton asked the woman.

"No." She pulled open the cell door. "You're free to go."

Shocked by her response, she searched the deputy's face. "What? Why?"

"Ask your attorney."

The woman turned and walked away. Afton followed, letting the deputy lead her through a maze of locked doors until she opened one into a nearly deserted waiting area. "There you go."

Corey stood and walked toward her. She'd never been so thrilled or surprised to see him, and she thanked the stars for looking out for her.

17

Afton stared into his concerned eyes, trying to make sense of how he'd found her, a town away in a jail cell. "Corey? What are you doing here?"

He pulled her into his arms, and Afton let him. After the uncertainty of the evening, she welcomed the warmth and safety of his hug.

"We heard what happened. I knew you'd need help."

She pulled back and shook her head in wonder. "But how? No one saw when Karl handcuffed me and threw me in the back of his car. He wouldn't give me a chance to tell Laurel or anything."

Corey rubbed his hands over her upper arms as though to warm her. "Someone did see, and they came into Sparrow's to tell Laurel. I called my cousin, who's an attorney in Pinecone. He convinced them it was in their best interest to drop the ridiculous charges before he filed a countersuit for harassment."

Welcome, soothing relief washed over her. "Oh, thank you. Thank you so much."

He studied her face, his expression one of concern. "Anytime, Afton. I meant it when I said you could trust me. I hope you'll believe that."

Something tender and hopeful blossomed inside her. "I do."

He gestured toward the front doors and held out a hand to her. "Let's get out of here."

She hesitated only a second before she took it and reveled in his strong fingers wrapping around hers.

Outside, Corey's beautiful pickup waited like a stallion in the olden days, ready for the hero to whisk the maiden off to safety. The romantic thought was silly, but the fact that Corey had driven to Pinecone and secured her release from the big, bad deputy wasn't lost on her.

He opened the passenger door for her and waited for her to climb in. She caught his gaze before he shut the door. "I can't thank you enough for this."

He grinned. "Are you sure? Because I wouldn't mind if you tried."

A flash of longing ripped through her. She shook her head as though to dismiss him, but she couldn't keep the smile from her face.

He raised his brows in a teasing gesture and shut the door. Damn if she wasn't in over her head, she thought as she watched him walk to the other side of the truck. How could she hope to continue to resist him?

Right now, that was a seemingly insurmountable mountain in front of her.

The moment he climbed into the driver's seat, the atmosphere changed, sparking to life with magnetic energy she couldn't ignore.

That was it. That spark. She'd felt it when they'd been together years ago, and it hadn't changed. If not for that, she could have walked away. Something about Corey Kendall compelled her beyond explanation and turned her into a woman who wanted nothing more than to be with him.

A tiny voice emerged from the depths of her conscience and

questioned why she *was* pushing him away. They were no longer immature teenagers, and he seemed to be as interested in her as she was in him.

She wanted to give him a chance. But she couldn't deny that doing so would likely bring more drama than she cared to have into her life. Most especially from her grandfather.

"This isn't the way I wanted to get you alone," he said as he started the engine. "But now that we are, there are things we need to discuss."

"Like what?"

He glanced over his shoulder as he backed out of the parking space, then paused and met her gaze. "Us."

Strong desire coiled inside her, and she swallowed. "*Us?*"

The truck bounced as Corey exited the parking lot onto Main Street. Businesses had closed for the day, leaving Pinecone looking more like a ghost town except for the few streetlights standing sentry, casting orange glows into the darkness.

He shot her a quick glance as he headed for the city limits. "Yes, us. I realize this is coming out of left field, but I want to get to know you better, Afton."

She paused as a multitude of thoughts raced through her mind. Foremost, she feared what her grandpa would say if she let Corey into her life. Grandpa was hard-headed, though if she presented things right, he could be reasonable.

Corey glanced between her and the road. "You're not saying anything."

"Sorry." She pushed out a breath, torn between her feelings and fears. "It's...umm.... You're very direct."

He lifted his chin. "I find it's the best way to communicate. I like to be honest. I feel as though you're a person who can appreciate that."

She wished she had the luxury of being the same without repercussions. She also recognized that any choice she made would have consequences, so she needed to choose paths that would be worth it. "Yes, I appreciate honesty."

"Good. That will be the base of our foundation. Not a bad place to start, wouldn't you agree?"

Afton hesitated, recognizing he was manipulating the situation, but she wasn't sure she minded. "Are you doing that thing where if you get me to say yes to two questions in a row, I'll most likely say yes to the third, the one thing you want me to commit to?"

He chuckled. "I love a smart woman."

She loved the intriguing tension hiding beneath their words. It had been the same when they'd lain beneath the stars. Her physical attraction to him had been undeniable, and still was. But she also enjoyed just talking to him.

She narrowed her eyes into a teasing gaze. "A vague answer combined with a compliment. I bet that gets you out of a lot of sticky situations, Councilmember."

His smile grew wider. "Actually, Miss Searle, if you examine our conversation, you'll find that you are the one who avoided the question, so let me repeat it. Honesty is a great base for our relationship. Don't you agree?"

A shiver of excitement rushed through her. "That's a trick question. I can't very well say no, but in saying yes, I'm agreeing we have the start of a relationship."

He reached over and took her hand. "Are you going to say no? Because, if you are, you should know I intend to change your mind, and I can be persuasive."

Warm strength surrounded her, and, God help her, she wanted more. "I have a feeling you wouldn't have much trouble with that. You seem to talk me into and out of all kinds of things."

His laugh rumbled through the cozy cab of his truck. "I'm glad you can appreciate my finer skills."

She definitely did. "Because you're so honest, I'm going to

surprise you and answer yes. Honesty is the best way to start a relationship."

He squeezed her hand and caught her gaze, as he slowed and then stopped at the side of the road.

"What are you doing?" she asked with a laugh.

"Something that can't be done with the truck in motion."

He leaned over and tugged her toward him until their faces were inches apart. His lips touched hers in a soft kiss that left her heart racing. A moment later, he scooted back and put the truck in gear again.

"I promise you won't regret giving me a chance," he said, his words echoing in the cab. He didn't look at her, didn't say anything else as he continued to drive. It was as though he didn't want anything to interfere with the seed he'd planted.

And it worked.

The taste of him and his promise were like water and sunshine, causing her heart to blossom. She knew she was messing with fire. Knew there'd likely be consequences. But her younger self begged her to give him a chance. Just a small, tiny chance to see if her intuition hadn't been wrong back then. She couldn't resist any longer.

Afton inhaled a nervous breath as she unbuckled her seatbelt and moved to the middle seat before buckling herself in again. She linked her arm through his and rested her head on his shoulder. Being close to him excited the hell out of her, but it also felt incredibly right. Her overactive imagination drowned out her common sense and told her they were meant to be.

For now, she'd accept what he offered. His scent of leather and spicy cologne caressed her senses as she breathed deep and closed her eyes.

She was safe. At least for the moment.

They stayed like that, connected and silent for the rest of the drive to Aspen. She didn't want to ruin the perfectness of the moment by voicing her doubts and fears. She wondered if he felt the same.

A half-mile from her house, he slowed and turned on a side road that led between two farmers' fields and continued down the lane. They traveled over the uneven dirt road, leaving a trail of dust in their wake as he increased the distance between them and the town.

"Where are we going?" she finally asked, her nerves twisting at the sight of the familiar road. She knew where he was headed, but why?

The engine in his truck shifted to a lower gear as the road sloped upward. He drove directly toward the small wooden cabin near the spot where they'd partied as teenagers. To the spot where she'd given him her innocence. "We need somewhere quiet where we can park and talk, where people won't see us."

The knots in her stomach tightened even more. "Grandpa will be worried that I haven't come home yet."

"Once we knew you'd been arrested, I had Laurel call him. You might get flack for getting too drunk tonight and passing out at her house, but he's not going to worry when you don't come home."

Which also meant she couldn't go home until morning. Still, it touched her that he'd worried enough to consider her circumstances. His actions had protected her and her grandfather.

Corey stopped when they reached the clearing in front of the old cabin.

"I haven't been here in years," she said, gazing at the weather-worn logs stacked in front of his headlights, as memories flickered in her mind.

She'd returned to their place one time, a week after they'd made love. The experience had been full of lovelorn angst, longing and regret, and it had hurt bad enough to chase her away for good.

Until now. "The cabin looks like it's sagging," she said.

The half-moon hovering in the sky provided the only light as he shifted in his seat. "Yeah. Not much can stand the ravages of time."

He paused for a moment before he spoke in a serious tone. "I know we were kids, Afton. We both jumped without thinking. But I need you to know I didn't take what happened between us lightly."

The noose tightened around her heart. "It was one night, and we never talked after that. It's okay. You don't have to pretend it was more than it was."

He held her gaze. "I'm not pretending. I'm not embellishing." He pulled her hand from her lap and folded it between his. "Let me explain it this way. I've dated many women, Afton. I've slept with *three*."

She blinked several times, processing the information.

"You were the first. I didn't want you to know that at the time because I wanted to impress you. All my friends had long since lost their virginity, and I was embarrassed that I hadn't."

Afton widened her eyes, shocked that she'd been his first, too. "Are you kidding me? I had no clue what I was doing, either. If it was memorable, it's more likely it was because of the setting, or maybe you were too drunk to realize how awful I must have been. Really. No one has good sex the first time around."

"Ouch." He paused for a moment and inhaled. "Okay. In my defense, I was a novice, but I'd hoped you'd enjoyed it on some level."

"No," she hurried to reply. "That's not what I meant at all. It *was* a magical night. The actual act hurt a little, but when we danced and then ran off into the night... And your kisses. You were so sweet. And I should really stop now." Before she spilled every feeling she had for him.

A hopeful smile curved his lips. "The point of telling you all this is I was still a virgin because none tempted me like you did. The other two after you didn't come close to how you made me feel. One night with you ruined me for other women. I know it sounds illogical, but that's how it is. I never thought I'd get a second chance."

He'd spoken the words she'd longed to hear. But now that he had, she was more uncertain than ever. "Honesty, right?"

She waited for his nod before she continued. She'd intended never to speak about that night, but here it was, staring her in the face again. "I've thought about you a lot over the years, even though I tried very hard not to. I really wanted to believe our night was special, but you made it clear afterward that it was a one-night stand. So, I did my best to put it behind me and move on. I get we were young, and I don't hold it against you."

He released a weighted sigh. "Trust me, Afton. I've learned much since then. I was a stupid boy. Not man enough to know what I had beneath my fingertips, still heavily influenced by family expectations, and drunk out of my mind. It doesn't excuse the way I treated you, but the lessons I learned helped me become the man I am today."

She lifted her gaze to his, wishing she had stronger light to read any unspoken thoughts that might appear in his eyes. "I guess we all live and learn."

"Exactly. Live and learn and not make the same mistakes twice, hopefully. I want to spend time with you, Afton, and rediscover the magic we found that night. Could you give me that chance?"

She blew out a tired breath, weary of all the what-ifs. "I might like that, too. But I'm worried. My grandpa will have a coronary when he finds out about us, and I can't add to his stress. Something's up with him, and I don't know what. I'd say he's having a mid-life crisis, but he's a little past that point."

"Health problems?" Corey asked.

She shook her head. "I don't know, but I don't think so. It's more his attitude. He's not the same hardheaded bulldog he's always been. Something has stolen his vitality, and I'm worried."

Corey chuckled. "That could work in my favor. He might be too distracted to hate me."

She narrowed her gaze and snorted. "Doubt it. He's not that far gone. He's already warned me to stay away from you. He's not too keen on your dad, either."

He frowned. "That's not fair. I'm a good guy. Don't you think he should meet me first?"

"Absolutely. But not with the way circumstances are right now. He has a problem with people in positions of authority. Always has as long as I can remember. He mentioned something about a past dealing with Mayor Gardiner, but he wouldn't give specifics, other than the mayor tried to swindle my grandpa."

"Laurel told me about Gardiner visiting you."

Her gaze jumped to his. "I wish she wouldn't have."

"Why not, Afton? You shouldn't keep anything like that quiet. I think you should file a report with the police."

She barked a laugh. "Right. They're going to believe the girl from the wrong side of the tracks over the Mayor of Aspen."

He shook his head in frustration. "Okay. You're right."

"And if my grandpa hears about it? It would either kill him, or he'd kill Dwight."

He nodded as though he understood. "Dwight spoke to me this morning, too. He made it clear he didn't like me kissing you in public."

She straightened her spine and frowned. "That's none of his business."

"That's what I said. Didn't stop him from threatening me or following through on his threat."

Unexpected fears brought goose bumps to her skin. "What do you mean, threats? What did he do?"

He swung his head to the side in irritation. "After I told him to butt out of my personal life, I'm positive he caused the Pinecone Planning Commission to drop me as the architect for their new administration building."

She turned more fully toward Corey, upset over his news. "He can't do that."

Corey hardened his features. "He did."

She placed a hand over her heart. How could Dwight be so cruel? "Oh, Corey. I'm so sorry."

"And now tonight with you being arrested? If you can't see a personal attack written all over it, I sure can."

She folded her arms and sighed. "Maybe you and I being together isn't a good idea after all."

He snorted. "Really? That's your answer? For some reason, I thought Johnny Searle's granddaughter would be a fighter."

His words, his tone, challenged her. "That may be, but a smart person also knows when to cut her losses. Now, it's not only me and my grandpa who are losing, but you, too."

"Some things are worth fighting for, Afton." He held her gaze, sending sharp electrical currents through her. "I'd like to conduct an experiment if you'll agree to play along."

She fought to switch mental gears as quickly as he had, but her brain was still stuck on the whole blackmail thing. "What?"

"An experiment. Don't tell me you're too cowardly for that, too."

She knew he baited her, but she couldn't back down. "I'm not a coward."

"Good." He slid his arm behind her shoulder, and his gaze softened. "There's something I want to prove to you, just in case you have any doubts."

He lifted a hand and cupped her face. She wanted to stop her heart from tumbling at his touch, but it was too late. Every bit of her weak reserve faded as he lowered his mouth to hers.

18

Corey smelled of leather and past longings, and Afton inhaled like she was taking her last breath. Passion exploded like dynamite. She was tired of denying what she felt, and she couldn't harness her feelings into submission if she'd tried. Couldn't tame the aching need to learn if what she'd imagined all these years was real or embellished by time.

She slid her fingers over his neck and into his soft hair, sensations whisking her back in time to their very first kiss beneath the stars. Heaven help her. She'd wanted him then, and she wanted him now. She couldn't fathom how something so powerful could have lain dormant for years, only to burst into existence once again.

She tightened her hold on him and tilted her head to deepen their kiss. He groaned and slipped the hand from her cheek, wrapping it around her and hauling her closer.

"Oh, God," she said as they broke apart, both panting. "That's..."

"It's good, Afton. Too good to ignore."

"Yes," she whispered as she sagged against the seat. "I can't pretend there's nothing there."

He cupped her chin, his face mere inches from hers. "That's what I needed to know. Nothing else matters. Certainly not what others think. I'll win your grandfather over eventually if you give me the chance. As for the mayor, it's only a matter of time before he goes down. I'll make sure of it, and I want you by my side when it happens."

Giddy hope rose inside her. "You're talking wild, you know? You're placing a lot on the line for a woman you don't really know. We've had only one physical night together and a few conversations since then, but that's it."

Corey dipped his head. "I recognize that, but know this, Afton Searle. I have an amazing ability to read people, to connect with them. I've never experienced a connection with anyone like I have with you. Now and years ago. It's not just sex. It's you. All of you."

She clamped a hand to her forehead at his unexpected confession, unable to process everything all at once.

He stole her hand and held it against his chest. "Unless you're going to tell me this is one-sided, which I wouldn't believe anyway, I'm not going to let you go without a fight. We owe it to ourselves to give this a chance, to see where it heads. Let's be crazy one more time and see what happens."

Excitement battled with her worries, creating utter chaos inside her head. Her heart threatened that it wouldn't allow her to let him walk away without giving them a chance.

His gaze pierced hers. "We might have opponents, but I'm not afraid to fight for something I want. Are you?"

Grandpa had raised her to be strong and unafraid. "I'm not a coward. But I think we should keep things on the down-low for a while. I don't want to risk messing up our fight for a business permit."

"That's probably for the best." He made a show of glancing at their surroundings. "But no one is around right now, so come here and let me kiss you again."

The decision to give them a chance chased away some of the dark clouds that had hovered over her. She had no doubt they'd encounter more trouble. But suddenly, the future seemed to have so many possibilities.

She didn't know if she'd trust her feelings in the morning, but right now, everything seemed more than right.

She gave Corey a quick kiss on the lips before ending it. She needed to cool things before they got out of hand. Not so much with him. But she didn't trust herself, didn't trust the aching need to touch him again that simmered deep inside her. "Let's get out. It's a beautiful night, and I want to look around." She pulled on the door handle and opened it.

"You're not going to see much in the dark."

She slid down, soft grass cushioning her shoes. A cool evening breeze, fresh with the scents of spring, curled around her, heightening her senses. "Leave your headlights on. It will be enough."

He nodded in agreement. "Yes, it will."

She strode toward the dilapidated cabin. "Remember the last time we were here? You turned up the stereo in your old truck, and everyone danced in the firelight."

She stopped not far from the doorway and glanced over the ground near the structure, looking for the spot where they'd had their raging bonfire. But the grass had taken over and buried all evidence of the past.

Without warning, he claimed her hand, as the lights from his truck cast their shadows against the rough-hewn logs. The breeze caught strands of her hair and sent them dancing. So much for creating a safe distance.

He tugged her, turning her to face him, and reached for her other hand. "I'll never forget that night. I'd been watching you for a while, you know? I was trying to decide if some guy with a green jacket was your boyfriend."

His touch left her with a shiver, and she fought to focus. "His name was Evan." One of her best friends from high school. His family had moved away while she'd been off at college.

"That's right, Evan Jones. He was constantly hovering around you."

She laughed. "We were just friends."

He cocked a brow. "If so, it wasn't *his* choice."

She tilted her head. "I'm pretty sure I know when a guy wants something more than friendship."

"You're wrong in this case." He pushed errant tendrils of hair from her face as he studied her features, wonder and interest heavy in his gaze. "When I finally claimed a dance, he was pissed. If his friends would have outnumbered mine, I think he would have done his best to kick my ass."

"Seriously?" She tried to remember any hint of attraction from Even, or a conversation about Corey afterward, but nothing came to mind. "I think you're mistaken."

He tugged her closer. "Yeah? I don't think so."

She probably should have resisted, but she couldn't.

"He didn't like the way I held you so close or when I kissed you."

His words sucked her into the memory of that first kiss, of how excited she'd been that Corey Kendall had not only noticed her. He wanted her. Just like he did now.

Dazed, she stared as he lowered his lips to hers and captured her mouth in a kiss that sizzled her blood. Without thinking, she drew her fingertips along his jaw, enjoying the raspy feel of his whiskers against her skin.

He paused, as if to study her reaction. She had her chance to push him away, but didn't move. "He probably wouldn't like us doing this then," she whispered.

"Nope." He tilted her head to the side and placed a trail of heated kisses down the length of her neck.

His tender assault was a tornado to her concerns, obliterating them and casting them aside. She gasped from pleasure and gripped his shoulders for balance.

"You smell good," he mumbled as he retraced the path of fire he'd created on her skin. "I just want to taste you."

When he nibbled her earlobe, she shivered. "Ah, God. Don't do that." Her response came out as a breathless whisper, and she realized too late that she shouldn't have revealed her weakness.

"What? This?" He tugged her hair until he'd exposed the opposite side of her neck where he did the same delicious things.

Her breaths deepened, and she savored the way his touch electrified and softened her body. Her nipples hardened in anticipation of his touch, and she pressed harder against him, needing to be closer.

Her mind tried to caution her, but she'd reached the point where her body controlled her actions. She wanted what she wanted, and they weren't hurting anyone.

He fumbled with the zipper on her jacket, unable to disengage it. She laughed and caught his bottom lip between her teeth, nipping and then soothing his skin with her tongue. He growled in appreciation before he straightened, leaving the evening air to cool her heated lips.

"Dammit," he said, his voice a strained whisper as he drew a finger along the curve of her collarbone. "You need to stop me."

"Why?" The breathless quality of his words echoed in hers.

"Because I can't do this. I don't want to ravage you under the stars and then leave you to wonder if I'll call again, but I can't walk away." He dragged his thumb across her bottom lip. "I intend to treat you like a lady this time and do things the right way."

Her body trembled. "What if *this is* the right way?"

He turned his face toward the heavens and exhaled a deep breath. "I promised myself the other night after you left that if I hadn't completely blown things a second time that I'd never give you another reason to doubt or mistrust me. I want this to be right, Afton, and I'm willing to wait to make sure it is."

The logical side of her latched onto his words with razor sharp nails. She *should* take her time, *should* be more careful with her heart.

But a powerful need consumed her. She retreated an inch and met his gaze more fully. "What if I don't want to wait?" She was primed and ready to give him her body at that moment.

He blew out an exaggerated breath and ran his hands up and down her arms. "You're not going to make this easy, are you?"

She chuckled, unable to resist the innuendo. "Actually, I'd hoped to make *it* hard."

"Oh, trust me. You have." He took her face between his hands and placed a gentle kiss on her lips. "Mmm. I can't tell you how much I'm anticipating the next time I touch you."

A fierce shiver rocked her. "But not tonight," she surmised. Part of her respected him tremendously for his determination. The other half wanted to ask what the hell was wrong with him.

"Does that mean you're looking forward to it, too?" he asked with a smile.

She groaned in frustration and took another step back. "I can't believe you're going to leave me wanting like this. What guy does that?"

Corey took her hands. "A guy who wants your heart as much as your body. A guy who knows you need to square things with your grandfather first."

The turn of events left her dizzy. "Are you saying I'm supposed to ask him if it's okay if I sleep with you? You're not serious. He'd pull a pistol and shoot you. Quite possibly me as well."

"Oh, hell, no. I'm not that stupid." He laughed and wrapped an arm around her, leading her to the truck. "But maybe you'd like a chance to give him a heads-up, let him know you're interested in me. We have time, Afton. Time to do this right."

Since when could a man make so much sense? "This is seriously messed up."

He seemed strong and steady, like someone who'd protect her. She wanted to lay her head on his chest and let him fold her into security, not to mention heated passion. But she had to be expecting too much. Considerate guys and sexy guys rarely came in one package. Could she really have found one so rare?

"I'd planned to talk to my grandpa tomorrow," she said as they reached the truck. After she made a trek to the hills. She had a good idea of the direction he always headed. All she had to do was follow the tire tracks. Depending on what she found there, she might have more than one thing she'd want to discuss with him. "If things work out, I'll mention meeting you. Though I'll be surprised if he hasn't already heard something about us with the way everyone is talking."

He gave her a sheepish smile that she didn't buy for a minute. "Sorry about that."

"No, you're not." She reached up to push away from his chest, but he trapped her hands against him.

"You're right. I can't be sorry for something I'll do again and again, every chance you give me."

She shook her head, unable to comprehend how fast things had changed. "Whatever. I just gave you a chance right now, and you turned it down."

He grinned. "Trust me, I know it. You have no idea how hard your sweet charms are to resist. I'm probably certifiable."

"No doubt." She exhaled. Despite her immediate disappointment, she understood and respected his intentions.

He tugged on a strand of her hair, a hopeful look in his eyes. "Are you going to talk to him in the morning? Can I take you to lunch afterward?"

"I actually have something I have to do in the morning first."

She considered telling him her fears about her grandpa, but

something held her back, despite their agreement to be honest with each other. Before she said anything, she needed to know everything she was up against.

If Grandpa was the man she feared him to be, Corey might rethink his decision to date her. What politician, with any hope for the future, would align himself with the granddaughter of a murderer? She swallowed her unease. "Can I call you in the afternoon?"

He smiled, his sexy lips turning upward, tightening the tension inside her. "Absolutely."

19

Corey dropped off Afton at Laurel's house to sleep for the rest of the night. Unfortunately, all she did was toss and turn on Laurel's uncomfortable couch. Possible future scenarios played over and over in her mind like an endless cycle of bad movies. None had happy endings.

When the sun finally rose, Laurel drove her home with her head pounding as though she really did have a hangover.

To the uninformed person, her life might seem perfect. She had a grandfather who loved and supported her. She was on the brink of owning her own business. Add to that, she'd attracted the man she'd always longed for, handsome, successful, and, most importantly, the one whose eyes lit up every time he looked at her.

Everything *should* be good. Wonderful, even. But beneath the calm surface, dark waters churned, stirring her anxiety, and warning her to beware of looming danger.

Proving to herself that her grandpa wasn't the infamous Johnny Searcy would go a long way in reassuring her that things would be fine. So that's what she'd do.

She breakfasted with her grandfather like usual, purposefully keeping her attention on the morning paper. Thankfully, he hadn't mentioned anything about her wild night and inability to drive home before he left for his weekly bullshit session with his gun club buddies.

The second his truck engine fired, she jumped up from the table, stopping long enough to drop her dishes in the sink. Sonny whined to go outside with her, but he'd already had a bathroom break, and she couldn't take him where she was going.

Outside, she strode across the gravel drive to the barn. The rusty hinges creaked when she opened it, and the familiar musty smell greeted her as she stepped inside and approached the four-wheeler. She hadn't ridden it in years, and she hoped it was still in good working order. It had better be because it was her only option to get up into the backcountry without her grandpa knowing.

She lifted her foot over the four-wheeler and straddled the machine. The key turned easily, and she checked to make sure the gear was in neutral. She pushed the starter, but the engine faltered, struggling for life.

"*Come on.*" She put on the choke and tried again. The four-wheeler coughed a few seconds and then fired to life. The motor sputtered when she turned down the choke, forcing her to wait while it idled for a few minutes before it would stay running.

With a prayer, she shifted the gear, and the machine moved forward. She stopped outside long enough to close the barn doors before continuing her quest for answers.

The long, bumpy dirt trail stretched ahead of her, taking her through stands of aspens with pretty green spring leaves. Guilt bounced along with her as she traversed the uneven earth and rocks, climbing slowly toward the hills. She should trust her grandpa, but she needed answers.

Not far into her ride, she reached the river, sparkling crisp and cool in the morning. Out here, everything seemed so peaceful. She wished her life could be the same. She paused, taking a moment to close her eyes to listen to the calming sounds of water moving downstream, promising herself she'd find the same peace in her life.

She crossed the area where the river spread out and flattened into a shallow drift of water, taking care to go slowly and not send water splashing into the air. She'd been known to do the exact opposite, and would have again today to relieve stress. But she might be out for a while and didn't want to be uncomfortable.

Years ago, when she was much younger, she'd gone for rides with her grandpa on the four-wheeler. She could remember gripping his denim jacket the first time they'd ridden, afraid she'd topple to her death if she let go.

He'd shown her the beautiful hills above his home, and she'd been thrilled when she'd spotted her first deer hiding in the pines. They'd discovered a cool cave, but he hadn't let her go inside any farther than the entrance while he'd checked it out. Not safe, he'd said.

They'd taken many trips after that, but there were many others when he'd insisted he needed time alone. She hadn't questioned his intentions then, but she did now.

He had to be making whiskey some of the time. No doubt about that. But what about the rest? Where could he have gone for hours on end? Perhaps he'd created a man-cave for himself where he could escape the realities of life and the drama of raising a teenage girl. The idea had its merits for her as well.

After the initial grove of aspens, the land leveled somewhat. She followed the dirt tire tracks permanently carved into the earth, letting the four-wheeler take her farther into the hills until she came to a fork. The tracks drifted off in three directions, and she was clueless about which to choose.

"Right is always right," she whispered, repeating her grandfather's infamous phrase as she shifted her gaze in that direction.

The trail wasn't particularly friendly with scratchy bushes growing next to it, but she had to choose one. Might as well start with it.

As she traveled down the dirt road, a sudden memory flashed in her mind, one of her grandpa clearing a path. Then another of him returning the debris to the same place on their return trip. "To avoid disturbing nature," he'd said.

She rolled her eyes as clues fell into place. "Horseshit." He'd been hiding something then, and he was still hiding it now.

Afton followed the trail until she found what she searched for, a pile of dead branches among the thick bushes. She stopped and climbed off the four-wheeler in order to inspect them closer.

She tugged on the branches, moving them to the side, revealing several black plastic pots filled with evergreen shrubs that grew naturally in the area. Anger for what he might be hiding replaced the worry she'd had for her grandfather. "I'll be damned."

There was the slight possibility that this was someone else's work, but these were her grandfather's mountains, and if a stranger was up here messing around, he'd know about it.

No, this was his doing.

Irate disappointment fueled her muscles and helped her clear the path within a few minutes. Ingenious, she thought, as she drove past the containers. No one would suspect another trail lay hidden beyond something that looked so natural. In the winter, when leaves were sparse, it would be more noticeable, but who came up here then?

Her irritation slowly faded to fear when the trail ended in front of a small cave. She shut off the engine and climbed from the seat, walking slowly toward the entrance. The line of demarcation between innocence and knowledge wasn't visible to her naked eye, but she could sense it as she approached.

Whatever she'd find in that cave wouldn't be good.

She pulled her cell phone from her pocket and turned on the flashlight as she approached.

The entrance was small, but she could see that the rock curved into a deeper recess. It had to be the same cave she remembered from her childhood. The one he'd explored without her.

Not this time. This time, she would know and see for herself how dangerous it truly was.

She stepped inside and was reminded how creepy and cold she'd thought it had been the first time. "Hello?" she called out. She didn't expect a human answer, but if a critter had taken shelter out of sight, she thought it might like to know it wasn't alone. She sure as hell wanted to know if she had company.

Nothing responded with movement or noises.

When she reached the curve, she realized why. Slabs of plywood blocked further entrance into the cave.

At that point, she thought about stopping, about returning home, and never mentioning what she'd discovered. As far as she knew, nothing was behind those boards. She could pull the petition and create new dreams back in Denver, ones where she flew solo, without her grandfather as a business partner.

She would lose Corey, but had she really ever had him, anyway? He wanted a relationship based on honesty, but honesty would be what would kill them.

Her tomorrows rested on what she'd find today, and she could no longer ignore the truth.

With one jerk, the boards fell to the ground, sending up a cloud of dust. Afton coughed and lifted her phone, shining the light around the cavernous room. "Oh, God," she whispered as she slowly walked forward.

20

Stacks of crates filled the small cavern, and Afton was certain about what they held. She worked the lid off the closest crate and lifted a bottle from inside. Clear glass showcased a rich amber liquid. Sagecreek Whiskey, 1998, had been handwritten on a white label in her grandfather's writing before being slapped on the front.

She replaced the bottle and pulled another that resembled the first. The crates looked to be full of them.

"Damn," she whispered as she glanced around. There had to be hundreds of bottles of illegal moonshine stored in the cave. Not just a few for the neighbors. The feds could put Grandpa away for years if they found out.

This is what her grandfather had been doing *every* damn time he'd left her alone over the years. He'd been making a shitload of whiskey.

She opened crate after crate, finding bottle after bottle until she came upon an odd-looking box toward the back of the cave. It was another wooden dynamite crate like her grandfather kept in the barn. Maybe *this* was where she'd find the information she sought.

She used her keys to pry off the lid and then sucked in a quick breath as she stumbled back. "Oh, shit." Her trembling hand caused the light from her phone to shake as she illuminated the contents. Red sticks of explosive lay quietly in the box, waiting like a coiled rattler to strike.

What did Grandpa intend to do with *that*? He'd buried the wooden box under bottles of whiskey dated 1970, and she wondered if he knew the dynamite was still there.

Disappointment slithered through her. Not just from her discovery, but also from what she hadn't found. She'd learned her grandpa had lied to her for years, but she'd come across nothing to prove or disprove his possible shady background.

Perhaps it didn't matter. What sat in front of her was enough for her to know they could never push their appeal any further. No wonder Grandpa had balked. He must have realized what would happen if they pushed too hard. He'd admitted to not expecting the mayor's reaction. If the mayor did as he said he would and called in the authorities, which she knew he would, she'd be visiting her grandpa in jail.

That was if they didn't haul her in as an accomplice. She gave a sarcastic snort. She'd already been arrested for solicitation, so why not this, too?

She replaced the boards and walked outside, needing fresh air to clear her mind. This changed everything. All her plans for the future. She'd never expected her grandfather to be perfect, but he'd been completely dishonest with her.

Or had he been completely dishonest *for her*?

He'd been a bachelor before she'd arrived, happy to live the simple life. Then suddenly, her parents had saddled him with baggage he couldn't have been prepared to support. She could only imagine what he must have sacrificed in order to raise her.

How often did he talk about wanting to leave her a legitimate inheritance? He'd constantly harped on her to get an education, to gain a strong mind so she could take care of herself because he wouldn't always be around.

She'd been the one to suggest they go into business together. Not him. He hadn't been on board until she'd pointed out how it would be the perfect solution to their problems.

They could use his expertise and the knowledge she'd gain at school to solidify both of their futures. The business would allow them to work together, and he wouldn't have to worry if she'd be okay.

She'd forced this on him. *She'd* pushed him beyond his limits. She had only herself to blame.

Now it would be up to her to make this right. To stop the petition. To tell her grandpa she'd changed her mind, too, and this wasn't worth it.

She'd need to find a job where she could support them both so he wouldn't have to continue to engage in illegal activity. It was unclear if she could make him completely stop, but if she lifted the burden from his shoulders, maybe he would slow down. As it was, he probably had enough whiskey between those stone walls to support them for several years.

She didn't want to insult his pride and his ability to provide for himself, but she needed to fix this before someone else did. It was far too dangerous to leave things as they were. She replaced the dusty boards and headed out.

Tension twisted inside her as she climbed onto the four-wheeler and turned the key. She pushed the starter, but nothing happened, not even a half-hearted buzzing noise. "No," she whispered.

She turned it off and then on again. Nothing.

"*Are you kidding me?*" She took a breath, trying to slow her pulse so she wouldn't overreact, and then she tried again. The engine remained completely silent. She glanced at the gas gauge, ensuring it still had fuel.

"Dammit," she growled as she climbed off. She reached for the pull-start and attempted to give it a jerk, but all her weight barely budged it. She paused for a moment to collect her strength and tried again, only to get the same results.

Why did it have to feel like the first domino had tumbled and the rest were going down no matter what?

She didn't want to call her grandpa because she needed more time to collect herself before the huge blow up she was certain would happen when she told him what she'd found. Laurel or her mom couldn't rescue her since they were women without a truck. Corey was the only one left.

He wanted honesty? Apparently, the fates were determined that's what he'd get.

She pulled her phone from her pocket and panicked for a quick moment until the screen assured her that she had service. She dialed Corey's number and waited, her heart pounding with thick, dull thuds.

"Afton," he said with a smile in his voice. "I was hoping I'd hear from you this morning. Have your plans changed?"

"More than I expected." She sighed, not able to see any good or happy way out of her situation. "I need your help. I'll explain more when you get here."

————

Corey followed Afton's sketchy directions, hoping he was on the right path. When he reached the tangle of branches spread across the roadway, they assured him he was. He had to stop long enough to move more tree limbs and potted evergreens to widen the opening and make it large enough for his truck.

Afterward, he continued following the tire tracks, and a few moments later, he found Afton sitting sideways on a dirty old four-wheeler not far from a cave opening, with an unhappy look on her face. He shut off his truck and climbed out.

"Hey," he said as he approached her. She looked damn good in ragged jeans, old boots, and a turquoise hoodie, so much that he couldn't resist the urge to hug her.

"Hi," she managed before he pulled her from the four-wheeler and into his arms. He kissed her soft lips, tasting of cinnamon this morning instead of strawberries.

He ended their kiss but didn't release her. "I'm sorry you've had trouble this morning. What are you doing all the way up here?"

"It's a long story."

He stared at the flecks in her green eyes, made even more noticeable in the bright morning light. "I like stories."

"Not this one." She flicked a glance toward the cave opening. "It concerns my grandpa and a not-so-welcome discovery."

He studied her expression, trying to discern her meaning. "Unless there are dead bodies in there, it's manageable."

A concerned look crossed her face, making him nervous. She inhaled a frustrated breath and blew it out. "I have to be honest. I considered not sharing this with you, but then decided what would be the point? If I show you, it will end us. If there even is an *us*. If I don't, it might prolong the relationship, but everything will come out, and you'll be forced to leave me."

He took a step back and grasped both her hands. "Why don't you show me and let me decide for myself before you predict the end of the world?"

She gave him a solemn nod before she pulled away and headed toward the cave. At first, the cave seemed like an everyday, normal rock structure until he saw the sheets of plywood. He held her illuminated phone while she removed them, and then she stepped aside.

"I'll be damned," he whispered as he stepped into the cavern filled with crates and looked around. "What's all this?" He noticed a large lantern sitting on top of a stack of crates, and he turned it on.

"Whiskey," she said as she came up alongside him. "He's been making it and storing it here for years. I knew he made some, but I thought it was just a few batches a year to share with his friends."

Corey gave a low-whistle as he made a quick guess of how many bottles of illegal whiskey sat in front of them. "Gardiner would kill for this information."

"I know," she whispered, sounding miserable. "I'm withdrawing the appeal for our permit. I can't imagine why my grandpa ever entertained the idea of starting a business with all of this hidden in the background. Unless he thought he'd never be caught. I need to do whatever I can to protect him. First, I must figure out a way to get all of this out of here before anyone discovers it. Worse, I need to decide how to tell him I've found out what he's done."

He turned and tried to comfort her with an understanding look. "Just be honest with him, Afton. It's the only thing you can do."

The low light enhanced the fear on her face. "It's not going to be easy. I'm sure he used this to make things better for us all these years, and I don't want to hurt him."

"No, but you have to protect him." He did another full circle view of the room. "You know, he must have another place besides this one. Where's his still? Unless he's cooking at home?"

She clamped her hands over her stomach as the color drained from her face. "No. I would have noticed if he was."

Corey retraced his steps until he emerged from the dank cave. He glanced around the surrounding clearing. To the left, he spotted something white through the thick covering of trees. Without hesitating, he jogged down a footpath leading through them.

"Come here," he called as he looked back, but he found Afton had already followed him.

"Oh, God," she mumbled before she passed him and made her way through the trees. She stopped and shook her head when they were in full view of a small white trailer hidden in the pines. "I can't believe this."

He had to admit he was shocked, too. He tried the doorknob, but it was locked. After moving to a window, he peered inside. "Damn curtains. I can't see anything. I wish we could get inside without breaking something."

Afton closed her eyes and whispered. "Check the top of the trailer for a key."

Her face had turned ashen, and she looked like the weight of the world rested on her shoulders. He pulled her into his arms and held her tightly. "It's going to be okay. No matter what happens, I'm in this with you. We'll figure it out."

She snorted. "No, you can't be. I'm worried this is only the beginning. What if this ends up much worse? If you're associated with me, it could ruin your career."

He smiled and shook his head. "If you think I'm worried about my political career, think again. Yes, it's a great opportunity for me to make a difference in the community, but I can find other ways just as well. Look at you and your puppies. My work as an architect will speak for itself. The mayor doesn't control everyone and everything around here, so please stop worrying about me."

Uncertainty deepened in her expression. "Just check the top of the trailer for the key, please. I need to see what he has inside."

21

Afton wasn't at all surprised when Corey felt along the top of the trailer near the door and returned with a tiny metal box with magnets on the side, which he handed to her. She opened it and removed the key. The pace of the world spinning around her seemed to slow, making sure she experienced every fearsome moment as she slid it into the lock and opened the door.

Stale, yeasty air surrounded her as she stepped inside, and she blinked a few times, trying to adjust to the dim atmosphere. Corey came in behind her, and she quickly glanced at him. He gave her a concerned look, but remained silent.

Two pressure cookers with copper tubing coming out of them sat on the stovetop. Along with that, two large metal containers rested on a solid board Grandpa had placed over the small bed in the front of the trailer. He'd covered both with cheesecloth and secured them with a large rubber band.

Corey scooted behind her and lifted a pressure cooker lid. "Nothing in here." He glanced toward the other containers. "What do you suppose is in there?"

"Mash."

He lifted his brows, surprised by her answer.

She lifted a trembling hand to her mouth while she gathered her wits. "He showed me how to make whiskey once, at home. We did it as a science project. Obviously, I couldn't turn in my results to my teacher, though, so Laurel helped me do another acceptable one at her house."

He nodded. "I see." But his expression said otherwise.

Her emotions barreled through the thin protective wall she'd created. "*You don't see.* You can't reasonably expect me to believe you understand any of this. You grew up in a normal household with a mom and dad who held respectable jobs. You could walk down the street without people making fun of you."

She tucked in her lips as she blinked back tears. "You can't have any idea what it was like to be raised by an older man, a recluse who thumbed his nose at society. You had someone to cook and clean for you. Your dad's friends were people like the mayor. My grandpa hung out with drunks and others who didn't conform to society's rules. I get why he did that now that I'm older, but it was hard when I was young. I wanted to be like everyone else, but I couldn't because my parents dumped me on a strange old man before they disappeared."

A deranged chuckle escaped her. "And now you want to date me? Are you kidding me?"

Instead of retreating like she'd expected, he stepped closer, taking hold of her arms just below her shoulders. His dark eyes penetrated hers, his expression one of serious intent. "I'm not going to insult you and say you didn't have a difficult time. I don't know what it must have been like for you, and I'm so sorry for your hardships. But I can say this. I'm glad you're not like everyone else. Your life experiences made you who you are today, a beautiful, sexy, vibrant, intelligent woman with a substantial amount of compassion for others, including puppies. So, while *you* might think your past and your family are black marks on your persona, *I* disagree."

She opened her mouth to speak, but nothing came out. She'd thought she'd have to defend herself further, but Corey had surprised her with his candor.

He filled his lungs. "Speaking of the supposed good influences I had during my childhood, don't forget what we've discovered about the mayor's true colors. He might look respectable on the outside, but his soul is beyond tarnished. On the other hand, I'd wager some of your grandfather's friends are wonderful people."

She blinked, ashamed of how she'd bashed on her grandpa's somewhat awkward friends. They had their share of problems, but they'd been the first to show up when their furnace went out on a wintry day and when her grandpa's truck had broken down. "They are good people," she whispered.

He dipped his head in a firm nod. "Right, so my next question is when are you going to get it through *your* head that I'm not the arrogant guy you thought and stop holding who I am against *me*?"

She stared at him, at his endearing face, gorgeous eyes and sexy smile, and the hammer hit home. "Oh, my God. You're not the judgmental one. *I am*." The thought troubled her deeply. Throughout her life, she'd harshly judged others for her current behavior.

He reached out and took her hand. "Why is it so hard to think I might like you for who you are? Do you think I don't know exactly who your grandfather is and what he's like?"

She snorted and circled her finger in the air. "I'm certain you didn't know he was doing this."

His mouth curved in a slight grin. "Maybe not to this extent, but more than half the town has drunk Sagecreek Whiskey. And it's damn good."

She wanted so much to believe him. "What if my grandpa is worse than we know? Worse than what we found today?"

She didn't want to believe he could commit murder, but it didn't seem out of the realm of possibilities anymore.

Corey laughed with derision. "It's quite possible my dad might have a whore hidden in the proverbial backroom of his life, so don't think we don't have any skeletons, either."

He turned her, pinning her against a storage closet. Gently, he took her chin and looked her directly in the eye. "This..." He touched his lips against hers, igniting a slow-burning flame deep inside her. "This is good, Afton. Don't let your fears chase it away. I did that when I was younger, and I've regretted it ever since."

She slid her arms around his neck and returned his kiss, allowing herself to melt into the lovely energy coursing between them. "Okay." She'd do her best to have faith in him and what he said.

He smiled down at her. "Good."

She bit her bottom lip as she stared at him, wanting more of his mouth on hers. More of the way his kiss, his touch, centered her world.

She traced her fingers along the stubbled line of his jaw before she stood on her tiptoes and captured his mouth. His kiss was soft, pleasurable, churning the need deep inside her. When he pulled away, she followed, trapping him against the stove in the tight quarters.

"I'm not done," she whispered. She needed to feel him. *All of him.*

She wrapped her arms around his solid torso, holding her body against his. Though he didn't fight her, she sensed the power lying dormant beneath her touch. She tugged the bottom of his soft cotton shirt upward until she had access to his bare skin. Shivers raced through her as she ran her fingers over his chest, eliciting a sexy groan from him.

"Afton," he warned.

"Let me," she whispered before reclaiming his mouth. She didn't want to wait. Didn't want to think. Only wanted to feel.

He did as she asked, letting her explore beneath his shirt. Smooth skin covered his lean torso and back. She traced the hard plains of his abdomen and the slight curve of his chest muscles. When she headed downward and slid her fingers beneath the waistband of his jeans, he tensed.

"You're headed into dangerous territory," he growled against her ear.

"I hope so."

She wanted to get lost with him in a wild wonderland. Stepping back, she tugged her hoodie over her head, knowing if she pushed him far enough, he wouldn't deny her.

He slowly shook his head as an entertained grin slid across his lips.

She nodded and pulled her camisole off next, exposing her lime green bra.

"Green," he whispered. "My favorite color."

"Mine, too." She turned and pressed against him, wrapping his arms in front of her. She placed his hands on her breasts and leaned her head against his shoulder. "Touch me, Corey. Please."

"Hell," he hissed. "You don't play fair."

Her agreement turned to a sharp intake of air as he molded his hands over her breasts, cupping her, massaging her, turning her nipples into highly sensitized buds. She arched, pressing against him, placing her hands over his as he caressed her. "I need this so much. Want you so much."

He kissed down the column of her neck and across her shoulder, sending waves of fiery quivers rocketing through her. The hard length of him pressed against her bottom, and she reached between them, needing to feel him.

He sucked in a breath and whipped her around, pinning her

against the closet again. "What are you doing, Afton?" Need burned in his eyes as much as it did inside her.

"Tempting you." She took a deep breath, which had the added benefit of attracting his gaze to her breasts. "Is it working?"

"Does it look like it's working?" He slid a finger along the edge of her bra and jerked it down, freeing her nipple. Before she could react, he sucked her deep inside his mouth, and her core tightened in a swift, sure response that stole her breath.

"Oh, my God," she whispered as she closed her eyes and gripped his shoulders.

He abandoned the first nipple, leaving it exposed as he repeated the same with her other breast. When she was heaving and dizzy, she tugged on his head, bringing his face close to hers. She gripped his hair and kissed him hard, needing him to know how much she wanted him.

He caressed her cheek as he pulled back and drew a thumb across her bottom lip. "I wanted our first time, the second time around, to be somewhere special. Not in a stuffy old trailer full of mash."

She wanted that, too. Glancing around, she spotted a folded brown flannel quilt tucked on a shelf. She took his hand, snagged the quilt, and headed outside. "Come with me."

She found the perfect spot near the trailer, and he helped her spread the blanket across a patch of meadow grass. They met in the middle. He took her hands as a soft breeze teased the air, and warm sun cascaded down through the new leaves onto them.

"You've totally bewitched me, Afton. I hope you know that."

She grinned, loving his words. "Have I now?"

"You know it." He drew a finger between her breasts, drawing a delicious shiver from her. "It's not a recent thing, either."

She closed her eyes, focusing on the sensation of his finger trailing across the swell of one breast. "I didn't know that part."

He reached around and unclasped her bra, baring her to all of nature. "I wished you would have. Wished I would have let you know how I felt back then. I tried to find you a few years ago, but you'd gone off to college."

She opened her eyes, caught his heated gaze. "It's okay, though, don't you think? Because we've found each other again?" Chances were, they wouldn't have made it if they'd tried to form a relationship right out of high school, anyway. "Now, we know who we are and what we want."

"True." He nodded as he popped the button on the top of her jeans. "And I want you."

A sweet tremble rolled through her. "I want you, too." She forced him to stop removing her jeans while she pulled his shirt over his head.

He started to wrap his arms around her, but she caught his hands. "Wait a moment. I want to..." She stepped forward until her breasts touched his chest, and then she slid against him, allowing her body to soak up the feel of him. Strong and warm. She sighed as he wrapped her in his embrace and gave her a long kiss.

His movements were slow after that. He kneeled and pulled down her jeans, kissing her hip through her lime green lace panties. Then her thigh. Then her knee, leaving her shivering from his touch.

She held his shoulders as she lifted her feet from her pants. The moment her legs were bare, he slid his hands up and down her skin several times, as though anticipating his next move. Then he pulled her panties from her body and kissed her inner thigh.

Her mind went hazy, and she was sure she'd die from need.

His fingers danced across her sensitive skin, and she tensed as he slid a finger along her folds. "Oh, God," she whispered as a small tremor burst inside her.

"You want me." He glanced up at her, and she nodded.

He tugged on her hands until she kneeled beside him, then he folded her softly to the ground. He quickly lost his jeans and underwear, exposing his magnificent body to her view.

She forced a breath as she gazed at him. Where he'd been lean years ago, he'd filled out with delicious muscle and confidence. His erection jutted out, filling her with sweet anticipation.

He took a moment to don a condom before he covered her with his large body. His weight settled on her like a heavy, safe blanket, leaving her wanting to play beneath the covers.

"Afton," he whispered and placed a lingering kiss on her lips. "I'm so happy we're here."

"Me, too, Corey. This is exactly where I want to be." She wrapped her legs around his waist, feeling him pressing against her core.

He kissed near her ear, nibbled along her jaw, before he found her lips once again. "I want to be inside you."

A strong yearning possessed her, and she shifted, trying to draw him in. *"Yes."*

He took her cue and thrusted. She gasped and arched her back as he filled her, not only physically, but emotionally, too. Heated sensations flooded her, and she held him tighter. A sigh full of exquisite pleasure slipped from her lips. "Yes," she murmured in his ear as he retreated and filled her again.

"Damn, Afton. I could lose myself in you forever."

She captured his face and stared at him as he pumped inside her. He watched her with wild eyes that dragged her deeper into the throes of passion.

She gave up with a gasp and allowed her eyes to flutter shut. The sense of him inside her and around her left her shaking. "Corey," she whispered as her need built to a higher level. What she wanted was just beyond her reach.

He slipped a hand between them and caressed her nub. Intense pleasure hit her like a rogue wave, knocking her into another dimension. She gripped his shoulders as multiple spasms rocked her core.

His soft chuckle brought her back to the beautiful mountain meadow surrounding them. "Are you okay?"

She gave an embarrassed laugh as she wrangled her mind into working order. "I've never experienced anything like that before."

He grinned. "Want another?"

"Most definitely," she whispered and rocked her hips against him.

22

Afton snuggled against Corey, the bright spring sun warming her body, making her drowsy. "I wish we could stay here all day," she murmured.

"Why can't we?" he mumbled against her hair.

"I need to return the four-wheeler before my grandpa gets home. He shouldn't be any earlier than four, but I can't be certain. I don't want him to know what I know. Yet."

Corey ran a lazy hand over her bare hip. "You'll need to have that conversation eventually."

"I know. But I don't want to spring it on him, not in the heat of the moment, not like, oh, hey, I went spying and look what I found. I need time to plan."

"Yeah." He pushed her to her back and partially covered her. "Promise me I can see you tonight. That's the only thing that will motivate me to move right now."

She stared into his beautiful dark eyes and wondered if she'd ever tire of looking at him. "Okay," she said with a laugh.

"You're easy to convince."

She wrapped her arms around his neck. "Only with you." She pulled him to her for a kiss.

They lingered for a moment, and then he rolled and helped her to her feet. They dressed except for Afton's hoodie, which she'd left near her grandpa's still. He folded the blanket and held her hand as they retraced the footpath.

Corey checked the four-wheeler while she headed for the oppressive trailer. Back to reality. Inside, she replaced the quilt and retrieved her hoodie, pulling it over her head and glancing about the room as she stuffed her hands into the sleeves. The constant sense of doom triggered her curiosity. Instead of leaving, she decided to peek inside the cupboards first.

Most were empty. Some held various supplies for the stills, and her grandpa had packed one with yeast and pounds of sugar.

She moved to the storage closet and tugged on the handle. It opened, and the scents of things stuffy and old wafted out. A worn sleeping bag sat rolled at the bottom while a flannel shirt hung from the lone hanger. She stood on tiptoe and slid her hands along the top shelf, but found nothing.

"What are you doing?"

She startled and then shot a glare at Corey. "Don't sneak up on me like that."

"Sorry." He chuckled as he surveyed the scene. "Looking for something in particular?"

"I'm not sure. Maybe old notes or documents." Links to John Searle's past that might provide more answers. "My grandpa mentioned the mayor had tried to swindle him at one point. I wondered if he had evidence of that, something that might protect us if he doesn't back down once I pull the petition. Maybe that's what the mayor wants from him."

Intrigue and mischief brightened his eyes. "Something to blackmail Dwight with?"

"Exactly." She opened another cupboard. Again, nothing.

"If you find anything, it might come in handy for me, too."

She'd be more than happy to oblige. "Will you check the top ones? I'm too short to see inside."

He did as she asked, but also came up empty-handed. "Are you sure he'd store them here?"

She sagged against the closet. "I don't know. I've searched other places, but honestly, I don't even know if such things exist. I keep thinking, though, with the way my grandpa keeps everything, there must be something somewhere."

He stepped closer and hugged her. "I'm sorry. Try not to worry. We'll figure this out. As it is, we should get going. I think the starter on your four-wheeler is shot, and I'm going to need some of those planks to roll it into my truck. We'd better hustle if we're going to beat your grandfather."

Frustrated and defeated, she turned toward the door. "You're right. I'd better tackle the issue in front of me right now. Worry about the rest later." She grabbed his hand, prepared to walk out, but he didn't follow along. She turned to find him staring at a cupboard above the stove.

"That's been altered." Corey pointed upward. "Look at that. The end cupboard should be bigger."

He moved closer and ran his hands along the bottom of the built-in storage space. "See this? One side is a good three inches wider. They don't design cupboards with unbalanced sides, and the section of faux wood next to it doesn't exactly match."

Afton stepped closer, now noticing the different sizes of both sides of the cupboard. "How did you spot that?"

"From studying architecture, I suppose. It's a necessary skill in my line of work."

His perception impressed her. "Maybe it wasn't manufactured very well."

"Yeah...not likely." He opened the cupboard and felt along the inside. "Bingo."

She couldn't see what he was doing, but suddenly he

produced a stack of papers and various envelopes, all held together by a rubber band. Dumbfounded, she took them from him, staring at her grandfather's hidden secrets. "It's like a birthday present and a bomb all rolled into one," she said. "I'm so excited that I'm shaking, but I'm worried about what I might find."

"We won't know until we look, but remember, knowledge is power. Whatever is in there is already the truth, has already happened. The only difference is we don't know what it is yet."

She looked at him, surprised at his depth of understanding. "You're so right. I need to remember that." Reverently, she undid the rubber band and placed it on the stovetop. The white envelope intrigued her the most, so she opened it first. Carefully, she removed and scanned the contents.

Slowly, she exhaled the deep breath she'd been holding. "Deed to the house and property. Nothing odious."

"Maybe it's all harmless."

She flicked a glance at him, wishing she could be as hopeful as he was. Next on the pile was a regular letter-sized envelope. She lifted it, but writing on the following manila envelope caught her eye. "Look. This one's labeled Dwight Gardiner," she whispered and met Corey's gaze.

"Wow. Interesting. May I?"

With her permission, he emptied the contents of the over-stuffed envelope on the small section of counter and opened a stack of tri-folded sheets. Air flew out of him like he'd been punched. "I don't believe it. These are documents from an investment business Dwight and your grandfather started over fifty years ago." He flipped a few pages. "It went defunct before they really got off the ground."

Afton pulled a thin notebook from the stack and opened it. "Oh, my gosh. This is a diary of all my grandpa's dealings with him. It talks about the amount of money he gave Dwight. How much Dwight lost." She turned more pages. "There's one entry here that talks about threats Dwight made against his life. Dwight apparently showed up one night, drunk off his ass, and, quote, proceeded to beat the shit out of me with a crowbar, end quote. *What?*"

Corey turned her so he could read over her shoulder. "He was arrested for assault and battery."

"Dwight has a record? Why didn't anyone know about that when they voted him in as mayor?"

He lifted a shoulder. "Maybe he had it expunged? His family has enough money and connections to keep something like that quiet."

"While Grandpa didn't and probably couldn't fight it." So unfair. She rifled through more papers, some of them legal documents, others newspaper clippings from the early years of Dwight's political career. "This is almost creepy. Like my grandfather is obsessed with him."

Corey shrugged. "Maybe he sees it as evidence of some sort. He even has a wedding picture of Dwight and...not his current wife. That's not Helen."

He held out the photo to her, and she took it. "Oh, my God. *That's my grandma with him.* I'm sure it is. Take a look. She looks like me."

"Damn," he said after a few seconds. "She does."

She blinked a few times, but the faces in the shocking picture didn't change. "That can't be. My grandma didn't marry Dwight. She married my grandpa. He keeps *their* wedding picture on the mantel."

Corey blew out a breath. "She must have married Dwight first and then divorced. Unless it's a hoax, but the picture looks legitimate to me. Look at the wedding gifts in the background."

Feeling dizzy, she made a beeline for the nearest padded cushion and sat. "I can't even..."

Her mind swirled, trying to reconnect the shattered pieces of what she'd thought was her family's history. *Her grandmother had married Dwight? Why?*

Corey strode closer and helped her up. "We should go. This is obviously something you need to discuss with your grandfather. I'll put everything back, and you can bring it up with him when you're ready."

"No!" She hurried forward and began collecting everything. "I'm taking this with me. My grandpa might see this as his business, but all this concerns me, too. And I want it with me when I talk to him."

Corey eyed her as though he wasn't sure, but he didn't argue.

After loading the four-wheeler in the back of Corey's truck, they headed out. The drive down the hillside was fraught with stiff silence. Neither said a word as they stopped long enough to replace the branches and evergreens. She couldn't get past her shock to carry on a conversation.

Thankfully, Grandpa wasn't home when they arrived. She climbed out of the truck without waiting for Corey to open her door, wanting to hurry things along as much as possible.

Together, she and Corey hastened toward the barn behind the house. She opened the door and entered the dim surroundings. Familiar musty scents greeted her, but she found no comfort in them this time. Her life had changed considerably, for the better and for the worse, ever since she'd headed out with the four-wheeler that morning.

Corey tugged the string on the overhead light in the entry, illuminating the surrounding area.

She headed toward the rear of the barn. "We have planks here, in the last stall."

Frustration hit her as she opened the gate. She whirled around. "I don't know why I'm so worried about the four-wheeler. So what if my grandpa finds out I was up there? He's going to know, eventually."

Corey walked forward and rubbed her arms before pulling her into an embrace. "Because you want to do this on your timeline, when you've calmed down and thought it through, remember?"

She soaked up his strength and released a large breath. "Oh, God. Okay. You're right. I can't lose my head over this."

He tilted her chin and gave her a soft kiss on the lips. "It's going to be fine, Afton. I have your back."

She nodded, letting a degree of calm flow through her. "Boards." After firming her resolve, she turned and entered the stall. She bent to pick up one end of a plank while Corey took the other.

"I've got this," he said after they'd navigated it out of the stall. He picked up the board, tossed it over his shoulder, and headed for the truck.

Afton turned to head into the stall to drag out the second plank, when she spotted an unfamiliar knapsack sitting haphazardly along the walkway. Her grandpa was worse than a kid.

She opened the bag and nearly died from shock as the triangulated head of a snake whipped out and sank its fangs into her hand before it retreated.

When she could find her breath, she screamed and dropped the knapsack.

Time and space distorted as a stinging sensation equivalent to a thousand bees attacked her hand.

Corey's voice sounded muffled as he hurried toward her. "*Afton?*"

She held out her left hand as dots of blood pooled on the surface of her skin near the base of her thumb. "A snake." Sweat broke out on her forehead, and she fought to keep her vision clear. "In the bag."

"Oh, my God." Corey rushed forward and buried her in his embrace. "It's okay. It's going to be okay."

"It hurts so bad," she said through her tears.

He scooped her into his arms, bouncing and jostling her as he ran from the barn. "Stay calm. Try to keep your heart rate low," he said in an even voice. "We're not far from a hospital."

He placed her in the passenger seat of his truck and disappeared into the barn again. A moment later, he threw the knapsack into the truck bed before racing to the driver's side and jumped into the vehicle. He had the ignition started before he completely shut the door. "Keep your hand lower than your heart."

Her thumb and fingers had already doubled in size, and the wound was turning a wicked shade of purple. "Oh, God. I'm scared, Corey. I can feel the venom inside me. It's making me dizzy and weak, and it's getting harder to breathe."

"Fuck." His tires spit a stream of gravel when he roared away from her house. "I know it feels really bad right now, but you're going to be okay. I promise."

He pushed something on the truck's console.

The sound of a woman's voice came through his speakers. "9-1-1. What's your emergency?"

"I'm en route to Uintah Medical Center from Aspen with a snakebite victim. A rattlesnake. Can you send an ambulance to meet us?"

23

A jangle of noises grew more distinct, and Afton began to differentiate the surrounding sounds. Corey's voice. A female voice...Joanna's. A constant beeping.

"Her pulse is strong," Joanna said. "No new swelling in the past hour. Ten appears to be the magic number."

Afton forced her eyes open and blinked several times against the bright lights. Her friend stood to the side of the bed, dressed in her nursing clothes. Her so-called surrogate mother lowered her injured arm and gave her a small smile. "Welcome back."

"Hey." Corey's voice came from the opposite side of the bed, and she turned in that direction. "You gave us quite a scare."

Her voice croaked as she spoke past her parched throat. "I did?"

Joanna poured water into a small plastic cup and handed it to her. Afton drank gratefully and then cleared her throat. "What happened? I remember the snake and driving here. At least part of the way."

"You went into shock halfway between Aspen and Pinecone." Corey squeezed her good hand, and she realized he'd been holding it all along. "Thank God the paramedics met us on the road."

Afton glanced from his tired face to Joanna's.

"You're going to be fine," she said. "We ended up giving you ten vials of antivenin to counteract the bite, along with antibiotics and a tetanus shot. Your injury is going to be painful, and it will take a while for the swelling to dissipate, but you'll be okay."

She didn't feel okay. She felt like hell. "I need to call my grandpa. To tell him what happened."

"He's already been here to check on you," Corey said, and then met Joanna's gaze.

Afton followed and caught the odd exchange between them. "Have I been out long?" she asked, trying to clue in on what she was missing. Had she come that close to death's doorstep?

"He was already here at the hospital," Joanna supplied. "Visiting me."

Afton glanced between the two of them. "Where is he now?"

"He should be here any moment," she said. "In the meantime, I'll leave you in Corey's care while I check on other patients and give the doctor an update on your progress. I'll be back soon. Ring the buzzer if you need anything."

Corey gave Joanna a reassuring nod. "I'm a permanent fixture while she's here, so don't worry about her."

After she left, he leaned closer to Afton's face. "Are you doing okay? Can I get you anything? More water?"

She shook her head. "No. Just sit with me if that's okay. I'm so sleepy."

"It's the trauma, the stress." He brushed her hair from her face. "Joanna said one of the meds they gave you might make you sleepy. Just rest."

"Okay." She so badly wanted to. "Someone needs to let Sonny out. And feed him."

He gave her a reassuring nod. "Lauren took him to her house."

That helped her rest easier. "Will you wake me when my grandpa comes?"

"Absolutely."

She wetted her dry lips. "Did he freak out when he found out I was with you?"

Corey chuckled. "Surprisingly, no. Don't worry about us, Afton. Everything is going to be fine."

She sighed and nodded as she closed her eyes, needing a few minutes of rest.

"*What the hell are you doing here, Dwight*?" The sound of Corey's hushed whisper brought her back around. "Come to see your work firsthand?"

"What the hell are you talking about, son?" Afton immediately recognized the mayor's voice. "I'd heard an ambulance had taken Ms. Searle and thought I'd check on her while I was in town."

She wanted to lift her lids, but she couldn't summon the energy. Corey would take care of him. She didn't need to.

"*Bullshit.*" The explosion of Corey's voice brought her eyes open.

The mayor puffed out his chest, looking affronted. "*Excuse me?*"

Corey stood taller. He lowered his voice when he spoke, but the anger remained. "I don't know who the hell you think you are, but this is going to stop."

Dwight took a step closer. "You're treading on dangerous ground, son."

Corey's body grew rigid with anger. "No, you did when you threatened Afton, telling her to watch out for snakes." He pointed at Dwight and then thumbed over his shoulder toward her. "Now she's in a hospital bed from a snake bite. Coincidence? I don't think so."

Dwight didn't bother glancing at her before he leaned closer to Corey. "I warned you all to back off, but don't blame this on me. I don't need to resort to underhanded tactics like this. I've already made several phone calls to ATF, and apparently, this time, I connected with the right person. An agent should arrive in Pinecone today. *That's why I'm here.*"

"You asshole." Corey grabbed Dwight's arm and jerked him out of the room.

Afton struggled to hear further conversation, but their voices faded away. "Dammit," she whispered as she fought to reach a sitting position.

She'd managed to get both feet on the floor but no farther by the time Grandpa walked into the room.

"Whoa." He held up a hand as he hurried forward and took her arm. "You trying to hightail it outta here, dumplin'?"

She had to tell him something, but what?

Her hand and arm throbbed, her vision swam, and her head pounded. As hard as she tried, she didn't have it in her to come up with a good lie. Besides, there had been enough of that as it was. "Dwight showed up, and Corey threatened to kick his ass." Her voice still sounded froggy, but it was stronger than it had been before.

"Good. If he don't, I will. Now, get back in bed." He forced her to lift her legs onto the mattress before he covered her with the thin blanket.

She didn't want to upset him, but she couldn't tiptoe around things any longer. "He thinks Dwight might have put the snake in the barn."

His tired eyes sparked. "Jesus H. Christ. *Are you kidding me?*"

She shook her head as an overwhelming sadness filled her. "He threatened me and Corey not long ago, told me I needed to watch out for snakes. He said I needed to force you to give him what he wanted or he would tell what he knew. Then today, I found the knapsack with the snake. It didn't just wander in there."

He shook his head repeatedly, his face turning red with anger. "The bastard probably meant it for me. He's been wanting to take me out for a long, long time."

"Ever since you stole his wife?" She shouldn't have said it, but she couldn't stop.

The color drained from his face. "Is that what he told you?"

Guilt washed over her in waves. "No. I came to that conclusion on my own."

"Then you'd better watch your mouth, missy, and not talk about things you don't understand. She left that son-of-a-bitching bastard. I didn't steal her."

She felt eight years old again, staring into the intimidating face of a man she didn't know.

But she did know him. He was her loving grandpa, and she refused to let this rift settle between them. "I would understand if you'd talk to me, if you wouldn't keep secrets. We're in this together, Grandpa. Why can't you trust me?"

He stared at her for several moments, and she recognized the look in his eye. It was the same one he always got before he took off.

"No," she said, lifting her hands. "Do *not* walk out that door."

Anger colored his words. "You're pushing me out."

She fought to sit up straight, but failed. "No, I'm not. I'm asking you to talk to me, to come clean."

He turned and headed for the door. "Yeah, well, I ain't talking."

"*Wait.*"

In a desperate attempt to stop him, she threw her legs over the side of the bed and stood. Instead of remaining upright, she crumpled, toppling the rolling side table as she fell. The lid popped off the pitcher, sending water running across the floor.

"What the sam hell are you doing?" He hurried forward and put his hands beneath her armpits and hauled her to her feet. "You're just as stubborn as your grandma."

Shaking, she allowed him to put her to bed once again. "If you try to leave," she warned. "I'm going to do the same thing all over again."

His hands shook as he righted the table and picked up the empty pitcher. "Dammit, girl. Stop messing with things you don't know about. Haven't you ever heard the saying about letting sleeping dogs lie?"

"But they're not sleeping, Grandpa. They're prowling, and if we're not careful, we're going to get bit." She cringed at her analogy. "You think things are fine, but they could be moments from annihilation."

His voice rose from stress. "Then burn the damn petition. I told you I don't want it anymore."

"It might be too late for that," she whispered.

He paused his fidgeting and met her gaze. "What do you mean?"

God help her. Here it was. "I mean, I know about your history with Dwight. I know about the cave in the hills and all the whiskey."

He shook his head several times, but didn't speak. Disappointment registered loud and clear on his face.

She gathered her resolve. "I wouldn't have snooped if you would have talked to me. But you won't. You slink around and keep your secrets. Damn, Grandpa. How many bottles are up there?"

He fixed his mouth in a rigid line that made her want to explode. "Enough."

"Enough? Enough for what?" She attempted to swing her legs over the edge of the bed again, but her grandpa held her down.

He met her gaze, his sharp and filled with anxiety. "Enough

that you won't have to worry about money if something should happen to me."

"Oh, Grandpa." She wrapped her arms around his neck and gave him a big hug. "You don't need to worry about taking care of me anymore. I'm all grown up. What I'm worried about is someone finding your stash and arresting you. I don't need you to take care of me. I need you here with me. Do you understand?"

Tears gathered in his eyes, and he coughed and turned away. It took him several moments to get his coughing under control again, but she couldn't harass him for still smoking right now.

"I worry about you," she said in a soft voice. "And I love you."

He sniffed and wiped away the moisture in his eyes. "I love you, too, dumplin'. I know I don't say it, but I'm happy your dipshit of a daddy left you on my porch. Besides loving your grandma, you are the best thing that's ever happened to me."

She chuckled to keep her own emotion at bay. "Even though I test your patience?"

"Even though." He took her hand and looked her directly in the eye. "I haven't lived a perfect life, Afton. I've done plenty of things I ain't proud of. But I've always tried to do my best to be a good grandpa to you."

"You are. The best."

She wanted to ask about John Searcy, but she didn't want to destroy what they'd just built if it was true. Now that they were talking, she would revisit the conversation another day. Soon, though. She didn't want anything buried any longer. She had more pressing things to worry about.

"Grandpa? We need to get rid of that whiskey. Like today. When the mayor was here, I overheard him tell Corey he was in Pinecone to meet an ATF agent."

His face paled. "*Son of a bitch.*"

His reaction twisted the tension inside her. "I'm so sorry. I've stirred up a hornet's nest with this petition, and I'm afraid Dwight's not going to stop."

Her grandpa released a deep breath. "It's okay, dumplin'. I'm not too worried. He ain't going to find that cave today, if ever. It's not like he can drive a sedan up into the hills. Even if he could, it's not easy to find. I've covered my tracks."

She thanked God she and Corey had replaced the pots and branches before they'd returned to the barn. "Still, it needs to go. We need to sell it or dump it soon, okay? Promise me that."

He studied her for a moment, and she could sense the wheels turning in his mind. She hoped he'd agree.

After a few moments, he nodded. "I promise I'll take care of it. They ain't putting me in jail, so don't you worry." He squared his jaw. "They won't find nothing of use up there."

That fighting spark he'd always carried jumped into his expression, and she wasn't sure if she was more worried or relieved. "You're not going to do anything stupid, are you?"

He laughed. "No, dumplin'. I'm not." He sat on the edge of the bed and held her hand. "Tell me about Corey Kendall. I thought you'd promised to stay away from him."

Hell. She should have known he'd bring the conversation back around to her. She shrugged. "He's not like the others, Grandpa. He's honest and loyal, and I think he's doing his best to represent all the people in Aspen. I know he's pissed off Dwight several times."

He chuckled. "Can't be too bad of a fellow, then, can he?"

Hope surged inside her. Maybe everything *would* be okay. "You wouldn't be angry if I dated him?"

"I could think of a few better men for you, but I'm guessing I don't have much say in that arena." He winked. "When your grandma and I hooked up, her parents weren't too happy, either. They liked Dwight's status, but she finally told them about the beatings, and then they supported the divorce. They never really warmed up to me, though. But at her funeral, her mother told me she was glad I'd made her daughter happy."

Afton swallowed around her constricted throat. "You miss her a lot, don't you?"

He wiped away more moisture. "Sure do. But I'll see her on the other side. I have you to keep me company until then."

She swiped her own tears. "Yes, you do."

"All right, little girl. I'd best be going for now. I've got plans to make. Joanna said they might release you sometime tonight or in the morning. Think that Corey of yours will give you a ride home?"

She smiled. "I'm sure he will. Maybe we can all have dinner together tonight?"

He gave her a wistful smile. "I'd really like to get to know him."

She wasn't sure what caused his melancholy expression. Maybe from missing her grandma. "You will, Grandpa. I know you'll like him."

He hugged her, and she kissed him on the cheek. "Love you, little dumplin', who looks so much like her grandmama."

"Love you, too."

She rested against her pillow as he quietly left the room. Maybe they could grill steaks for dinner. Corey was an expert grill master, along with so many other things.

24

"Afton!"

She awoke with a start at the sound of Corey calling her name. He stood next to her, his expression frantic. She blinked several times, trying to get her bearings. "What's wrong?" Besides the fact she was still at the hospital.

"It's your grandfather." He strode to the closet and pulled out her clothes. "We have to get you dressed. Have to get out of here."

The tension in his voice brought her wide awake. "What happened? Is he all right?"

"It's not good." He tugged at the tie on her hospital gown before handing her bra to her. "The last thing I want to do is drag you out of here, but he might need you. He's barricaded himself up in the hills somewhere. I'm going to guess the trailer. Dwight and an ATF agent are headed there now, expecting to ambush him just after dawn, I think."

"No..." she whispered as an overwhelming sense of doom buried her like a landslide. She tossed her bra aside and pulled on her hoodie. It hurt like hell to shove her injured hand through the sleeve, but she didn't care. "If they push him, I'm afraid of what will happen."

She stood and paused until the dizziness and nausea settled. "Let's go." She strode right past the nurses' station, not knowing or caring if she'd been released.

Her grandpa was in trouble, and she'd be there for him.

As they left the medical center, the sun barely crested the horizon, giving the morning a rosy kiss. Corey had an arm around her, helping to keep her steady. A quiet chill hung in the air, but that wasn't what left her cold. "I knew something wasn't right when Grandpa left. We talked about you, and I wanted us all to have dinner together when I left the hospital. He didn't say no, but he didn't exactly say yes, either, you know?"

Corey sent her a worried look but didn't answer. When they reached his truck, he opened the door and helped her in before he raced to the driver's side.

Though it hurt every time she moved, she scooted on the seat until her thigh touched his. She needed the reassurance of feeling him next to her.

Her thoughts tumbled between hopeful and fearful as they sped toward her grandpa's house. "How did you find out about this?"

"From a friend who works as an EMT at the sheriff's department. He was called in as a backup."

Her blood pressure dropped, making her dizzy. "They've called EMTs? Are they expecting to need them?"

Corey squeezed her hand. "Have faith. That's why I snatched you, to help diffuse the situation."

A bone-trembling shiver coursed through her. "I don't know. When he gets like this, there's no telling what he might do. Especially if they force him into a corner. If they've found the whiskey…"

She couldn't finish her sentence, couldn't stop thinking about the crate of dynamite she'd discovered.

Corey drove past the house and barely slowed when he

reached the dirt road leading into the hills. Her teeth chattered as he cruised over the ruts, making her head hurt worse from all the jostling.

When they approached the area where her grandpa had camouflaged the road to the cave, she could see the bushes and evergreens had been cleared away, exposing the worn trail. She covered her mouth with a trembling hand. *"No."*

"Shit," Corey hissed in agreement.

A blockade of emergency vehicles forced Corey to stop his truck. Afton struggled to see beyond the red and blue flashing lights but couldn't. She thrust open her door and hurried forward, ignoring the throbbing in her hand.

A group of uniformed men hovered near the rear of an SUV with one man holding a bullhorn. Early sun rained down on them. If the beautiful area, full of pines and aspens, hadn't been marred by officers with guns, it would have been a spectacular morning.

She headed off on her own, taking an alternate path toward the cave, away from the officers, but Aspen's sheriff caught up to her and grabbed her by the arm before she cleared the first vehicle.

"Let me go," she shrieked. "That's my grandpa in there."

The older man with kind eyes and strands of silver in his dark hair shook his head. "I can't let you do that, Afton. Too dangerous."

She struggled to pull away, but he held firm. "Are you insane? He's not going to hurt *me*."

The sheriff slowly shook his head. "He has one hostage in there already. I'm not about to give him two."

She grew unsteady and would have fallen if Corey hadn't caught up in time to catch her.

"Morning, Councilmember," the officer said to Corey.

"Morning, Sheriff Reynolds."

She ignored their greetings. "Who is it? Who's in there with him?"

"Mayor Gardiner, ma'am."

"Oh, God." She turned to Corey, shaking her head multiple times. "This isn't happening. I must get in there. I'm the only one who can stop this."

"I can't let you go," Sheriff Reynolds said. "But I'll let you talk to him. Maybe that will help."

Corey supported her as the sheriff led them to the group, where he commanded the attention of his officers. "For those of you who don't know, this is Afton Searle. Johnny's granddaughter. She thinks she might help by talking to him. See if you can get him to answer again," the sheriff said to an unfortunately familiar deputy before he shifted his focus back to her. "He's been refusing to communicate with us for the past ten minutes."

Karl sent her an angry glare before he dialed. He appeared to listen for a few moments and then shook his head. When he spoke, he nearly snarled. "If your grandfather harms one hair on the mayor's head, he's a dead man."

"Shut up, Karl. You're already in deep shit." The sheriff took the bullhorn from another of his men. "Johnny, this is Sheriff Reynolds. I'm here with your granddaughter, Afton. She wants to talk to you. When we call again, pick up the phone." He nodded to Karl, who repeated his earlier steps.

This time there was an answer on the other end, and Karl held out the phone to the sheriff, who snatched it like a lifeline.

"Johnny, listen to me," Sheriff Reynolds said. "We're here to help."

The senior officer remained silent for a couple of seconds. "Okay. I'll put you on speakerphone like you've requested." The sheriff pushed the button and held out the phone.

"Grandpa?" Afton said, tears making her voice tremble. "Are you okay?"

"Okay as I can be, dumplin'."

She wrapped her arms tightly around her, barely feeling the pain in her hand. "Please come out. We can find a way out of this. I need you."

"Is the mayor okay?" Sheriff Reynolds asked.

"He's fine," John Searle said. "I'm sending him out in a minute, but I need to say a few things first."

Relief flooded Afton. "Thank you, Grandpa. I love you."

"I love you, too. Okay, here's what the rest of you need to know. Mayor Gardiner is a liar and a cheat, and he physically abused his wife. He's managed to keep most of this hushed for years. I knew it, but I stayed out of his business because he stayed out of mine. Until now. Now, he's gone too far. I believe my granddaughter has all the documentation that will prove these facts."

All eyes turned to her.

She hesitated and then nodded. "I think I do. I haven't looked through everything yet, but I'm in possession of my grandfather's papers."

Her grandpa cleared his throat. "When you read them, Afton, just remember how much I love you."

"Grandpa—"

"The mayor's coming out," he said overtop of her words, creating a commotion around her.

She picked up the phone and took it off the speaker, needing to have a private moment with him before whatever would happen, happened. "It's just me, now, Grandpa. I love you. Please know how much I love you."

His voice sounded ragged. "I do, dumplin'. I do. Don't let them read everything, okay? Let's keep some of it between me and you."

She wasn't sure what exactly he referred to, but she couldn't deny him. "I won't. I'll only give them stuff about the mayor."

"You say that Corey is a good man?"

She glanced at Corey, who watched her with concern burning in his eyes. "He is. A very good man."

"That's all I need to know. Remember, it won't be long before we see each other again."

His words gave her hope. "Okay. I'll see you soon, Grandpa."

The line went dead.

"The mayor's coming," someone shouted.

Afton released a breath and met Corey's gaze. "It's going to be okay."

She barely finished her sentence before the ground beneath her shook with a violent rumble as hell broke out on earth. Massive flames burst from the cave, sending the officers into a raging frenzy.

"*No!*" Afton screamed as she watched her world end.

Corey caught her and held her. She pushed, trying to free herself, and then sagged against him, as a piercing wail surfaced from the depths of her soul. Not her grandpa.

Not her dear, beloved grandpa.

25

Afton sat in Grandpa's rocking chair on the back porch, staring at the gorgeous hills rising beyond her. The vivid orange sun, midway through its descent, cast a fiery glow on the green hillside. Peace emanated from everything around her, but it couldn't penetrate the powerful ache consuming her heart.

Fresh tears started anew, and she swiped at them. Her grandpa had been gone less than twelve hours, and yet it seemed like a lifetime. How would she ever make it through the first day? Or the second?

Things shouldn't have ended like they had. If the authorities hadn't cornered him, trapped him like an animal, he'd still be alive. She would have kept his secrets, taken them to her grave.

She slid the remaining newspaper clippings and another of his diaries back into the manila envelope and fastened the clasp. She tucked them under the blanket with her, swearing she'd find a better hiding place than he had.

Of course, it wouldn't matter now if people knew his history. He was dead. They couldn't prosecute him for killing another man. And he wouldn't have to worry whether he could prove he'd done it in self-defense.

He didn't have to worry about anything any longer.

A sob fell from her lips, and she pulled her legs up against her chest, curling into a ball. He'd gone out on his terms, she reminded herself. A final "up yours" to the world who'd never been especially kind to him. He'd be with her grandma now, celebrating, and she'd try to be happy for that.

"Hey," Corey said as he came out the back door. He caught sight of her tears and hurried forward. He kneeled in front of her and gathered her into his arms. "Oh, honey. I'm so sorry."

She struggled to gain control of her tears. "Is it always going to hurt so much?"

He pulled back and wiped the moisture from her cheeks. "It'll get better. Give time a chance. It has a miraculous way of healing, or at least, filling in the hole so you don't notice the pain so much."

She inhaled a shaky breath and nodded, afraid if she spoke, she'd start crying again.

He studied her with a concerned gaze. "I met Sheriff Reynolds in town and gave him the papers and your grandfather's journal. There's enough in there that Dwight will be forced to step down from office. Sheriff thought there might even be enough to convict."

She shrugged. "I hope so, but no matter what happens, it won't bring my grandpa back."

"I know." He nodded. "My mom sent some soup."

Afton blinked several times, her lashes wet against her cheeks. "She did? For me?"

He chuckled and nodded. "Yes, for you. She's concerned. She'd like to visit, but she wasn't sure how you'd feel about it."

She shook her head, feeling dazed. "I thought she'd hate me."

He shrugged. "She has no reason to hate you."

She sniffed. "Your dad will. He's Dwight's friend."

Corey scoffed. "My dad was shocked when I told him what we'd discovered. I think he's going to lie low for a while. He admitted he'd lost money by investing with Dwight a few times, too, but Dwight always came up with a good story. I think he'll be doing some investigating of his own."

He pulled a chair over and sat next to her. "Sheriff asked if I'd given him everything we'd found."

She widened her eyes. "What did you tell him?"

He took her hand and squeezed it. "I told him that was all there was. He said your grandfather made it seem like more, but I reassured him. In the end, I believe he was satisfied."

"You lied." She couldn't have been more grateful.

"Yes, and no. We gave him everything that was pertinent to this event. He didn't need pictures of your grandparents together, the ones of you when you first came to live with him, or anything else from your grandfather's past."

A half-laugh, half-cry escaped her. "You sound like a politician."

He joined her with a chuckle and helped her to her feet. "I am. I hope you can live with that because I plan to be in your life, starting with tonight. I'll stay here, or you can come to my place, but I'm not leaving you alone."

"Thank you," she said and wrapped her arms around him.

"Hello?" a female voice called from inside the house.

Corey met her gaze with lifted brows, and he held her hand as they walked through the back door.

Joanna and Laurel stepped into the kitchen just as they did, and Laurel rushed forward and buried her in a hug. Afton's crying started again, and Laurel and Joanna joined her.

Corey dished up soup and cut bread while the women shared their grief. "If you all could sit and eat with Afton, that would be great. She hasn't had anything all day."

"Yes," Joanna said and forced Afton into a chair. "I have something to tell you, but not until you've had a few bites."

Afton ate some soup and half a slice of bread before she looked at Joanna with an expectant gaze. "I know you loved him," she said to the other woman. "He loved you, too."

"Not like he loved you, missy. He worshiped the ground you walked on. He constantly talked about how you reminded him of his wife."

She lifted her brows. "He talked to you about my grandma?"

The look in Joanna's dark eyes switched to bewilderment. "Of course. We were friends. Why wouldn't he?"

She shrugged, feeling awkward. "I thought he...liked you."

Joanna snorted while Laurel tucked her auburn hair behind her ear and leaned into the conversation.

"Oh, honey. You thought..." Joanna laughed again. "Your grandpa loved to flirt with me, but he only ever loved your grandma."

She shook her head, feeling confused. "But it seemed more than friendly visits, and don't tell me it was so you could buy whiskey." With everything she'd lost, she deserved to know the truth.

Joanna released a long sigh as her expression saddened. "That's what I wanted to talk to you about. I know you're sorely hurting from what happened today. I hope what I have to say will help and not make things worse."

Afton blinked rapidly, trying to keep her tears at bay, as she struggled to guess what she might say. Corey took her hand.

Joanna held her gaze for a moment and then nodded. "Afton, your grandpa was dying. He was undergoing treatment for stage four small cell lung cancer. His prognosis wasn't good, and his doctors gave him less than a year. More likely, much less. I came by as often as I could to check on him."

Afton placed a shaking hand over her mouth as she processed the information.

"*What?*" Laurel asked, obviously shocked.

Corey shook his head. "Wow."

Afton inhaled and then exhaled as she replayed events since she'd come home. "He never said anything."

Joanna sent her a comforting smile. "No. As much as I tried to get him to tell you, he refused. He said he was meant to take care of you. Not the other way around. He always told me he'd be gone the moment he couldn't take care of himself, anyway. Afton, I believe this was his way of deciding what happened to him. The ATF agent's arrival was the catalyst that set events in motion, but he'd already intended to take his own life. He wouldn't have allowed you or him to suffer through his illness."

"Oh, God." She put a shaking hand to her chest. "I can't even..."

"I know, honey." Joanna shook her head, looking disturbed. "I didn't want to add to your stress, but you needed to know. Your grandpa should have told you."

She nodded, unable to speak.

The older woman stood and gave Afton a hug. "We should go. You need to rest."

"You'll take care of her?" Laurel asked Corey.

"Absolutely. I have no intention of leaving her alone."

"Good." She wrapped her arms around Afton. "Don't worry about Sonny. He's a good boy. I'll call *you* in the morning. You call me if you need anything, and I mean *anything*. Will you be okay?"

Afton nodded, though inside, she couldn't be sure.

When they'd departed and the house was quiet again, Corey tugged her to her feet. "My house or yours?"

"I'd like to be here."

He gave her a gentle smile and nodded. "Good thing I grabbed my toothbrush."

EPILOGUE

Afton bounced along the highway in her grandpa's old, rusted truck. She'd lowered the windows, letting in the sweet smells of summer, and she'd cranked up the music, singing along with the old Willie Nelson cassette her grandpa loved so much.

She could have borrowed Corey's truck, but driving Grandpa's old blue Ford into Pinecone to pick up the massive bags of donated dog food gave her the opportunity to remember the man she loved so dearly.

Three months had passed, and she still missed him desperately. But, as Corey said, life went on, and she'd found a way to be happy again. She'd be forever grateful for the sacrifices her grandpa had made for her and the things he'd taught her. She'd decided she'd show that gratitude by going on to have a good life. It's what he'd want.

Dwight, however, would likely live the rest of his days in misery. John Searle's notes and allegations led to an investigation that not only cost him his mayorship, but the respect of the town, and the possibility of jail time for scamming Aspen's residents on more than one occasion.

Karma, she supposed.

Either way, she no longer cared. She wished Grandpa could have been around to watch the fallout. He would have enjoyed it, but maybe he and her grandma were watching from somewhere else, too.

She liked to think so.

As Afton rounded a bend, the sight of a small ginger-furred body sitting off to the side of the road caught her attention. She slowed and then pulled to a stop.

She left the truck running as she climbed out and wandered to the other side. There, sitting in the grass, was a too-skinny cat with huge green eyes. It meowed, but didn't move.

She approached carefully, unsure if it was feral or not. Then she caught sight of the dirty red collar around its neck and knew it had belonged to someone. She kneeled next to the cat and held out her hand. "What are you doing way out here? There aren't any houses for miles and miles."

It released a loud holler, but rubbed its chin against her fingers. She gently picked it up. "You're so skinny. Are you lost? Did someone leave you here?" She glanced around, though she didn't expect to find any answers to her questions.

Vibrations from the cat's purrs soaked into her body as she ran her hand over its dirty fur.

"That's settled then, Ginger-kitty. You're coming home with me. Hopefully, you have a microchip, and we can find your long-lost owners. If not, I'll make sure you have food and a warm, safe home."

She climbed into the truck and set the cat next to her on the seat. It immediately climbed onto her lap and settled in, continuing to purr.

Fifteen minutes later when she pulled in front of her grandpa's farmhouse, she was delighted to see Corey waiting for her.

She climbed from the truck with the cat firmly tucked into her arms.

He laughed and lowered the truck's tailgate to unload the dog food. "Another one?"

She petted him between his ears. "I couldn't leave him on the side of the road. Look how hungry he is."

"How do you know it's a boy?" Corey lifted a heavy bag to his shoulder and headed toward the barn.

Afton followed. "There's evidence of his boy-kitty parts," she said with a laugh.

Several puppies barked as they entered the musty barn, but the ginger kitty didn't tense in the slightest, and she hugged him tighter. "I think he must have grown up around dogs, too. He's not scared at all."

She set the cat on the ground, and it followed her as she retrieved bowls of food and water. The second she put them on the ground, the poor kitty chomped away.

Corey came up behind her and wrapped his arms around her waist. "You're a kind soul. Do you know that?"

She shrugged. "I do what I can."

"Which is more than most." He twisted her until she faced him. "I saw Scott and Katy Beckstead in town with Sonny, who doesn't look like much of a puppy anymore. He had his head hanging out the passenger window, looking like he owned the world."

Happiness lit inside her. "He's such a sweet doggie. I'm so happy they love him."

Corey tipped her chin up. "Not as much as I love you. Which reminds me, I have a surprise."

She grinned. "What is it?"

He took her hand and led her outside to his truck. He cast a sly glance at her before he opened the passenger door and retrieved a stack of folded documents. "Here."

She drew her brows in question, but was unable to keep the smile from her face. Carefully, she took the papers and unfolded them. The official Aspen City document had been signed and dated by the council. "Permit to Operate" stood in bold letters at the top.

"*What is this?* Sagecreek Distillery?" She met his gaze. She'd given up that dream when her grandfather had died. "I can't believe you all approved it after all."

He laughed. "I don't know if you still want it, but I put the petition through during the last council meeting. You'd already done the work. Getting the permit was a formality, but it's yours if you want it."

She put her hand over her mouth as her dream resurrected. "It's going to be a lot of work to get it up and going."

He gave her an encouraging look. "It will. But you have all your grandfather's recipes. The nest egg of investments he left you would help get it off the ground financially, and I'd be interested in investing in your future as well since I intend to be a part of it."

She glanced at the engagement ring flashing on her finger, the tears in her eyes making it extra sparkly. "Okay, yes." She met his gaze, her heart beating faster. "I'd like to try it. I would really like to honor his life by cooking up some whiskey...the legal way."

"Good." He cupped her face and gave her a heated kiss. "I see many good things for us, the future Mrs. Kendall. No doubt there will be some crazy ones, too."

She grinned. "That's okay. I've decided I like crazy."

Afton tugged his head to hers and kissed him, ready to get on with the rest of her wonderful life.

I hope you enjoyed Afton and Corey's love story. Read on for an excerpt from I'm With You, the next in the Aspen Series.

. . .

Sign up for my newsletter to receive notifications of new releases, freebies, and special sales at www.CindyStark.com. Also, if you have a moment, I'd appreciate a review!

Thank you very much, and happy reading!
   Cindy

PREVIEW: I'M WITH YOU

1

Zoe Cassidy glanced down each aisle of Randall's Western Outfitters as she walked around the country store, searching for packing tape. Mr. Randall had an odd way of categorizing items. Power tools hung next to women's socks, and apparently, adhesives and toilet plungers belonged together. The citizens of Aspen often joked about his system, but Zoe suspected it was Mr. Randall's way of keeping people in the store longer, hoping they'd buy more stuff.

"Ha," Zoe muttered when she spied the adhesives and turned her cart in that direction. If the day went according to plan, she'd have everything except her big furniture moved into her new, turn of the century house by evening. Finally, a place she could call home, a luxury she'd never enjoyed until now.

She was halfway down the aisle when Asher Campbell entered from the opposite way, and she screeched to a halt.

Why?

She asked the same question each time she had the unfortunate experience of running into him. In a town as small as Aspen, she should probably consider herself lucky that she didn't bump into him more often. But every time she did...*ugh.*

She might have gotten over past hurts and her damned attraction to him if he'd gone bald or gained a gut during the ten years since high school, but he hadn't. If anything, he looked better. Ripped jeans showcased powerful thighs. Dark hair peeked from beneath a dusty ball cap. His broad shoulders could certainly carry the weight of the world if he wanted.

And those eyes. Those stormy gray eyes that peeked from beneath his lashes when he'd watched her. He was probably dreaming up the next awful remark he'd say to her.

Didn't matter. *He* didn't matter. She was beyond that era of her life. She'd get her tape and leave. No need to speak a word to the obnoxious man.

The moment she moved faster down the aisle, he glanced up.

She quickly shifted her gaze as though she hadn't noticed him and focused on her targeted supplies. But out of the corner of her eye, she caught him striding purposefully toward her.

Why couldn't he leave her alone?

Their carts nearly collided as they both stopped in front of the packing tape. "Afternoon, Zoe. Long time, no see."

Even his voice was sexy with deep resonating sounds that affected her more than she cared to admit. She truly hated him.

With a quick glance in his direction, she acknowledged his presence. She couldn't find anything nice to say, so she said nothing at all. Instead, she snatched two rolls of tape and dropped them in her cart.

"Are you finally moving out of Olga's basement?" Asher asked when she didn't answer. "What a dump. I don't know how you stood to live there that long."

She frowned as his insult bored deep into her soul. It wasn't like she'd *enjoyed* living in a dark hole with an eccentric lady as a landlord. But a single girl, whose mother had taken off to God-knows-where many years ago, couldn't afford to be too choosy.

Emotional words clawed their way up her throat, and this

time she opened her mouth. "Do you always have to be such a jerk?"

He widened his beautiful eyes as though surprised by her remark. "I didn't mean it like that, Zoe."

That's what he always said after insulting her in whatever fashion suited him at the moment. It was like some weird bait and switch routine he used on her. Insult her and then deny it. Not this time.

She tossed her invisible shield between them and curved her lips into a chilled smile. "Have a nice day, Asher."

Then she turned and walked away.

Dammit. She'd sworn the last time she'd encountered him, she wouldn't allow him to push her buttons again. But he'd managed it so easily. Why?

What was it about him that gave him power over her, that allowed him to cut her so easily with careless words?

She shook off her annoyance and focused on the day ahead. She needed to get to her new home and start cleaning. Old Man Jenkins hadn't left it in the best state, and she had work to do before she could move in. Still, if she put her frustrations into her work, she'd be too busy and too tired to think of anything or anyone else.

First, she had one more stop to make before she headed home. *Home.* Her home.

Yes.

———

"Dammit." Asher watched the one woman who stirred his blood like no other walk away. *Why?*

Zoe's loose blond curls swayed as she walked with a grace that contradicted her backwoods, redneck upbringing. Even in their younger years, when she'd been all knees and elbows, she'd exuded a natural beauty that he hadn't been able to ignore.

It was unfortunate that she'd turned out to be full of piss and vinegar instead of sugar and spice and everything nice. Not that he could blame her, but...

"I see you're still charming the ladies," Seth Moore said as he approached.

Asher fired a glare at his long-time friend and recent business partner. "Whatever."

Together, they'd started their own business and had currently built nearly a third of the new houses in town that year. He cared far more about that than a sassy woman, no matter how pretty she was.

The blond construction worker chuckled. "You're the only guy I know who's managed to piss off a woman just by existing,".

He turned to Seth. "Right? What the hell is up with that? She's hated me for years, and what did I ever do to her?"

Seth shrugged as he readjusted his ball cap, giving Asher a glimpse of flattened blond hair. "Women. Who can figure them out?"

He pulled a roll of packing tape from the shelf. "Not me. That's for damn sure."

Especially after his ex-wife had kicked him out of their home months ago. She'd needed to make room for the new man in her life, and Asher had been in the way.

He still couldn't quite stomach that.

Thank God, he'd finally found somewhere to live. Luckily, he wouldn't need to pack much since most of his stuff was still in boxes.

His friend tested the weight of the hammer he carried. "Honestly, I'm not sure why you care. If Zoe can't be nice, who needs her?"

Asher stared at his friend, letting his words drill home. "You're right. I've tried to be friendly. If she can't do the same, something's wrong with her."

Even as he said it, he regretted it. He'd known of her struggles through childhood. He'd admired the strength she'd shown when others had made fun of her because her clothes were outdated. Or when she was late because her mom had been too wasted to drive her to school. She'd let the teasing roll right off her back and get on with whatever she'd been doing.

He scrubbed the short whiskers on his chin, remembering the many times he'd fought hard to gain enough courage to talk to the elusive, quiet blond beauty, to tell her what he thought of her. But his tongue had always tripped him up and he'd say some stupid shit like he had just now. Then she'd leave him standing like a lone fool.

Different variations of the scenarios played through his head, all with the same outcome. Maybe he'd never understand women, as evidenced by his recent divorce. Really, what the hell did he care about *any* of them?

"What time do you want me to show up tomorrow to help move your stuff?" Seth asked.

Asher had been camping in his friend Milo's spare room for the past few months, but he'd grown tired of intruding on him, his wife, and their new baby. When an old friend of his mom's mentioned he'd thought of selling his place, Asher had been all over that. It would be quiet and on the outskirts of town. The perfect place to mend a broken heart.

He jutted his chin at Seth. "Be there around nine?"

Seth lifted his chin in a decisive nod. "You got it, buddy. By the way, I saw Dana the other day. She wanted me to ask you to back off on making her pay you for your share of the equity in the house."

Anger scratched at him like a bare tree branch in a windstorm, constant and annoying. "What did you say?"

"I told her it wasn't my business, and I wouldn't get involved."

Asher paused and then nodded. "Thanks, man."

The thought of his ex-wife and their messy divorce was still a potent source of pain for him, and any mention was a cattle prod in an open wound.

He'd aired the dirty trash left over from his marriage to Seth and Milo many times over too many beers. Thankfully, they'd supported him like brothers.

After a time, he'd realized he could bitch about his circumstances all he wanted, but it wouldn't change anything. What was done, was done. Continuing to talk about and dwell on how badly Dana had treated him only served to bleed his pain and prevent his heart from healing.

Seth clapped him on the shoulder. "Hang in there. Having your own place will make it better. You can work on fixing up the old house when you want, and sit around in your boxers all day and drink beer when you don't, and no one will say a word."

A semblance of a smile hit his lips. "Yeah." There was that to look forward to.

ABOUT THE AUTHOR

Award-winning author Cindy Stark lives in a small town shadowed by the Rocky Mountains. She enjoys writing about forever love with hot men and strong women in her sexy contemporary romances, along with penning unexpected twists in her emotional romantic suspense stories, and creating magical mayhem in her paranormal cozy mysteries.

She'd like to think she's the boss of her three adorable and sassy cats, but deep down, she knows she's ruled by kitty overlords. Someday, she hopes to earn enough to open a cat sanctuary where she can save all the kitties and play all day with toe beans and murder mittens.

Connect with her online at
www.CindyStark.com

ALSO BY CINDY STARK

ASPEN SERIES (Small Town Sexy Romance):

Wounded (Prequel)

Relentless

Lawless

Cowboys and Angels

Come Back To Me

Surrender

Reckless

Tempted

Crazy One More Time

I'm With You

Breathless

PINECONE VALLEY (Small Town Sexy Romance):

Love Me Again

Love Me Always

ARGENT SPRINGS (Small Town Sexy Romance):

Whispers

Secrets

BLACKWATER CANYON RANCH (Western Sexy Romance):

Caleb

Oliver

Justin

Piper

Jesse

RETRIBUTION NOVELS (Sexy Romantic Suspense):

Branded

Hunted

Banished

Hijacked

Betrayed

COOKIE CORNER COZY MYSTERIES (PG-Rated Fun):

Cookie Calamity

Haunted Cookies

Cursed Cookies

Conjured Cookies

Killer Cookies

Shadow Cookies

SWEET MOUNTAIN WITCHES COZY MYSTERIES (PG-Rated Fun):

Midlife or Death

For Once in My Midlife

One Midlife to Live

Midlife in the Fast Lane

Midlife of the Party

Such is Midlife

Mysterious Midlife

Love of my Midlife

Merry Midlife

CRYSTAL COVE COZY MYSTERIES (PG-Rated Fun):

Murder and Moonstones

Brews and Bloodstone

Curses and Carnelian

Killer Kyanite

Rumors and Rose Quartz

Hexes and Hematite

TEAS & TEMPTATIONS COZY MYSTERIES (PG-Rated Fun):

Once Wicked

Twice Hexed

Three Times Charmed

Four Warned

The Fifth Curse

It's All Sixes

Spellbound Seven

Elemental Eight

Nefarious Nine

Hijacked Honeymoon

A Witch Without a Spell

Mystical Mayhem

WITCHES OF PORT TOWNSEND (Sexy Paranormal Romance):

Which Witch is Which

Which Witch is Wicked

Which Witch is Wild

Which Witch is Willing

OTHER TITLES:

Sweet Vengeance

Moonlight and Margaritas